NO PLACE LIKE HOLMES

NO PLACE LIKE HOLMES

JASON LETHCOE

THOMAS NELSON®
Since 1798

NASHVILLE   DALLAS   MEXICO CITY   RIO DE JANEIRO

Published in Nashville, Tennessee, by Thomas Nelson. Thomas Nelson is a registered trademark of Thomas Nelson, Inc.

Thomas Nelson, Inc., titles may be purchased in bulk for educational, business, fund-raising, or sales promotional use. For information, please e-mail SpecialMarkets@ThomasNelson.com.

Page design by Mark L. Mabry

Library of Congress Cataloging-in-Publication Data Pending

ISBN 978-1-4003-1721-9

Printed in the United States of America

12 13 14 15 QG 15 14 13 12 11 10

For Alex and Olivia Rose

Affliction is often the thing which prepares an ordinary person for some sort of an extraordinary destiny.

—C. S. Lewis

CONTENTS

CONTENTS

ABOUT THE WORLD'S MOST SECRET DETECTIVE

"How did Griffin Sharpe get his limp?"

"Did he really meet Sherlock Holmes?"

"What about his gold pocket watch? How did he get that?"

"Is it true that he carried a walking stick that belonged to the greatest villain in history?"

These are just a few of the many questions people ask me about the great detective Griffin Sharpe. And because I've spent over thirty years researching and collecting everything that is known about his life and adventures, I am thrilled to finally have the opportunity to write down his story, starting at the beginning. For his adventures began a long time ago, when he was just a boy, long before he became the famous detective we all know.

Sometimes, when I'm at a speaking engagement or book signing, other fans share a rumor or piece of information about him that I haven't heard. I can't tell you how exciting it is to find out some new little fact that I didn't know, or to be shown an item that Griffin Sharpe used in one of his adventures.

I try to post these discoveries regularly on my blog: noplacelikeholmes.blogspot.com.

I welcome others to share their findings too. Between us, I'm sure we can unravel the mystery surrounding Mr. Sharpe, "The World's Most Secret Detective."

For those of you who have never heard of Snodgrass and Sharpe, welcome! And for those of us who have followed their adventures closely, hearing them wherever and whenever we could, much of the content contained in this book is familiar.

Until now, none of these incredible adventures have ever been written down. Due to the great secrecy that Mr. Sharpe insisted upon over the years, many of his adventures were largely unrecorded. They've been passed down through the generations by word-of-mouth, the firsthand accounts of witnesses who saw the great detective at work.

However, I was recently honored to receive special permission from Dame Victoria Sharpe to transcribe the wonderful stories you are about to read. Ms. Sharpe is currently eighty-nine years old and has asked that I preserve her father's legacy in print. It is with great humility that I have attempted to do so.

So sit back and imagine what it was like to live a long time ago, back when motorcars were rare and pianos tinkled in elegant parlors, when men wore top hats and ladies carried beautiful parasols.

Welcome to the year 1903.

JASON LETHCOE
NOVEMBER 2010

PROLOGUE

Frederick Dent removed his beautifully engraved pocket watch from his vest pocket. As he opened the lid, the sound of "Westminster Chimes" tinkled softly in the early morning air.

Five fifty-seven a.m.

He snapped the watch shut with a *click*, cutting off the music, and gazed out over the misty banks of the River Thames.

This is ridiculous, he thought. The strange client who had walked into his London shop two days earlier had insisted on meeting him here to deliver for repair what was promised to be one of the rarest clocks in Britain. Frederick had been so excited about seeing the clock that he hadn't thought about the oddness of the request until he was on his way to the famous river. The client had requested that Frederick be there, at this exact spot, at six o'clock sharp. But why couldn't he have brought the clock to Frederick's shop like any other normal person? It just didn't make any sense.

Frederick shivered and pulled up the collar of his tweed jacket. The fog that surrounded the banks was unusually thick. He sighed and decided that the whole thing was probably a prank. After all, the client *had* acted rather suspiciously. Frederick had deliberately ignored the fact that the man had kept the lower half of his face carefully hidden beneath a scarf, and now he regretted it. At the time, he thought the stranger must have had a head cold.

I'll wager it's those Reilly brats, he thought. The urchins were always trying to steal from his display of pocket watches when he wasn't looking. After catching them at it last week, he'd threatened to call the police. Perhaps they'd convinced a beggar to act the part of a rare collector, arranging this little trick as an act of spite.

Shivering in the miserable drizzle and trying to hold his breath against the fishy stench in the air, Frederick decided that it was time to give up waiting and go back home to his wife. She was sure to have a nice pot of tea brewing, and if he were lucky, the scones she had been baking would still be warm.

A sudden noise in the water interrupted his thoughts. Frederick looked around for what had caused the bubbling noise. He was surprised to see that the water looked as if it were boiling not forty meters from where he stood.

What the deuce?

Without warning, a slimy, black head followed by a long, serpentine neck rose out of the water. Frederick stared, eyes wide with shock, as the monster let out a terrible roar.

James Dunn, a local fisherman, arrived just in time to see the great beast snatch the terrified clockmaker into its jaws. Then, with a quick *gulp*, the monster swallowed Frederick

Dent whole. The fisherman let out a terrified cry and ran from the shore.

All that remained on the muddy riverbank was Frederick Dent's golden pocket watch, which had popped open as it fell to the ground. The ripples from the monster's departure into the Thames lapped against the shoreline, keeping time with the gentle sounds of "Westminster Chimes" that tinkled in the mist.

The watch finished playing the famous melody, and its tiny bell chimed six times.

A SHARPE BOY

Griffin Sharpe noticed everything.

When people spoke, he noticed the color of their teeth. He also counted the number of frayed threads on men's shirtsleeves or the number of feathers on a lady's hat. And he didn't just notice that they were there. He also carefully noted the color and the type of bird that had supplied each one.

He memorized entire sections of the Bible, *Webster's Dictionary*, and the *Encyclopedia Britannica*, and could recall any part of them when he needed to. Everything he saw was photographed with his mind's eye and stored for use at a later date. In other words, Griffin Sharpe was one of those rare individuals whom people refer to as a "genius."

But even though he was incredibly smart, Griffin was a humble boy. His father, who was a Methodist minister, had taught him that the sin of pride was the basis of many others. And Griffin did his best to resist the temptation to correct others when they were wrong. He'd found out quickly that being right all the time didn't help him make friends.

In fact, one of the main reasons Griffin had traveled all the way to London from Boston was because he hadn't been invited to spend the summer at a local camp with his schoolmates. The other children hated him for being the teacher's pet. Answers to questions seemed to pop into his head before the schoolmaster had even finished asking them, and it was hard for Griffin to contain his excitement when he saw the solution to a problem. That never went over well with his classmates.

Griffin had the bruises to prove it.

He gazed around the tiny train compartment in which he now sat, his sad, blue eyes taking in all the details. He was alone; the other three seats in his compartment had been empty for several stops. Griffin had just finished counting the number of tassels on one of the velvet window curtains when the brass-trimmed door slid open and a friendly man's face appeared.

"Ticket, please."

Griffin reached into his coat pocket and removed his ticket. As he handed it to the conductor, he noticed that the man wore round brass glasses that were called Pince-nez, that one side of his handlebar moustache was waxed and curled more tightly than the other, that he had a spot of Dijon mustard on the left side of his jacket's lapel (probably from his lunch), and, most strangely of all, that the edges of his shirt cuffs had dirty, gray marks around their edges.

All of these things Griffin noticed in the split second before the conductor had torn his ticket. Everything about the man was acceptable and ordinary in Griffin's opinion, but the man's soot-stained shirt cuffs gave him pause. Then, as the man handed back his half of the ticket, Griffin quickly deduced an explanation.

"Oh . . . excuse me, but has the train been shorthanded today?" Griffin asked politely.

The conductor hesitated, appearing confused. "Excuse me?"

Griffin smiled and indicated the man's sleeves. "I don't mean to be rude, sir. I was just curious since I happened to notice the soot marks on the edges of your cuffs. I assumed that perhaps you might be helping with the fireman's duties, shoveling coal into the engine's firebox. The coal dust on your sleeves indicates that you probably weren't wearing gloves."

The conductor gave Griffin a long searching look and then burst out laughing. "My word, young man! You're a regular Sherlock Holmes!"

Now it was Griffin's turn to be confused. "I'm sorry, but I don't know who Sherlock Holmes is," he said.

In response, the conductor reached into his back pocket and pulled out a rolled-up pulp magazine. Handing it to Griffin, he said, "Mr. Holmes is the greatest detective in the world. Everybody in London reads about his adventures in the *Strand Magazine*. My wife can't get enough of them . . . waits in line every Tuesday to get the next installment."

Griffin flipped through the beautifully illustrated magazine quickly. One of the pictures caught his eye almost immediately. It showed the famous detective standing in front of a modest brick building.

The address was 221 Baker Street.

Griffin gasped with surprise. He glanced up at the friendly conductor and said eagerly, "But that is precisely the address to which I'm heading. I'm going to visit my uncle!"

The conductor studied him with a curious expression. Then with a chuckle, he said, "Well, as I live and breathe. Wait until I tell my wife that I met the nephew of Sherlock Holmes. She'll be so excited that she might faint right there on the spot."

Then, after giving him a friendly wink, the man ducked back out of Griffin's compartment. The boy sat staring at the magazine, overcome with excitement. He'd never met his uncle before, but his mother had always referred to him as Snoops, a nickname she'd used since they were children. He'd never heard her say his real name, so Griffin had to call him Uncle. After all, calling a relative he'd never met Uncle Snoops seemed a little strange.

Could it be possible that his uncle was the same great detective that the conductor had mentioned? He knew that his uncle and his mother were half brother and sister, so it was possible they had different last names. He studied the picture of Sherlock Holmes, noting his tall, lean frame and angular profile. If he squinted at the picture, he thought the man did resemble his mother's side of the family a little.

Filled with anticipation, Griffin settled back into his seat and began to read. And the more he read about Sherlock Holmes, the more excited he became. For here was someone with a mind not unlike his own, someone who observed even the smallest details and was helping people with his talent.

For so long Griffin had prayed that God would give him an opportunity to use his talent for good, and that he could find a friend as well. He'd asked Him to help him find somebody who wouldn't make fun of him and call him names for being smart.

And finally, after a very long time of asking, he'd received an answer to his prayer.

THE CONSULTING DETECTIVE

But you don't look anything like Sherlock Holmes!" the woman exclaimed, waving her copy of the *Strand* in his face. The scruffy man stared back at her with an annoyed expression. After a moment he sighed and rubbed a tired hand across his forehead.

"No, madam," he replied, forcing a smile. "I never claimed anything of the sort."

She was right, of course. The man knew exactly what Mr. Holmes looked like, and he didn't resemble him in the slightest. Rupert Snodgrass had seen Holmes's arrogant, hawkish profile and his triumphant smirk too many times to count. The mere thought of the detective sickened him.

"Mr. Holmes lives next door. You're at 221A Baker Street. You'll find him at B just over there." He indicated the door next to his that led to the upstairs apartment.

As the woman turned to leave, the man couldn't help introducing himself. "Forgive me, madam. But my name is Rupert Snodgrass, and, as unlikely as it may seem, I'm also a consulting detective."

He smiled wide, displaying all of his teeth with the hope that he could entice her to stay. Since she hesitated, he pressed on. "Actually, you'll find my rates just as reasonable as his, if not more so." Mr. Snodgrass winked, hoping that being friendly would make her feel that he was making a special exception just for her.

The fact was he desperately needed some business. He had been living on a small tin of stale biscuits for over a week and was dangerously close to being kicked out of his flat. This might not have been such a bad thing, considering that he happened to live next door to the world's most famous detective and had competing businesses. But he was determined to stay and not allow his neighbor to destroy his dreams of becoming England's most famous detective himself.

Rupert Snodgrass was not going to take defeat that easily.

If the woman heard his offer, she didn't show it. She whirled from where she stood and without a second glance backward was at his neighbor's stoop. Seconds later she was being ushered into Mr. Holmes's apartment by Dr. Watson.

Snodgrass scowled. After slamming the door shut, he stomped back into his study. The cup of tea that had been prepared from old tea leaves was cold. Disgusted, he dumped the murky liquid on top of one of his numerous wilted houseplants and went down the hall to his bedroom.

He cleaned his teeth while gazing into a small, cracked mirror. The man with a receding hairline, red-rimmed eyes, and an unshaven beard who looked back at him seemed defeated. Then, with a depressed sigh, he toweled off his face and climbed into bed.

As he lay there, staring at the ceiling, he realized an

important truth: people with elegant surnames like Sherlock and impressive features to match inspired confidence in their clients. Since when, he wondered, had a "Rupert Snodgrass" ever amounted to anything but a fishmonger or a tailor? He didn't look the part of a great detective, and he knew it.

His head ached, fueled by anxiety over his unpaid rent, his lack of success as an investigator, and indigestion from moldy biscuits. Snodgrass felt sure that if he could just solve one case before Sherlock Holmes, his entire life would turn around. He lived with the hope that one day it would be *him* staring back with a triumphant grin on his face as the newspaper reporters took down the story of how he solved the mystery before his neighbor did.

Oh, what sweet revenge!

While on the last case, the one with the cursed dog that haunted the Baskerville moor, he'd nearly done it. But, like most things in life, coming in second place just wasn't good enough.

The delicate strains of a violin playing a perfect Mozart concerto filtered down from the apartment above. He could imagine his neighbor's long fingers caressing the strings, creating music that was beautiful and pure. There seemed to be no end to Holmes's maddening talents. Rupert Snodgrass grabbed the broom from the corner and pounded on the ceiling as hard as he could, shouting for quiet.

But Sherlock Holmes didn't stop playing.

THE ARRIVAL

The following morning Snodgrass was awakened by a sharp, insistent rapping at his door. He flung back the sheets with a bearlike growl and, after grabbing his dressing gown, stomped to the door. Seizing the handle he yanked it open, expecting, for some irrational reason, to see Sherlock Holmes standing there.

But it wasn't Holmes. Instead, a boy of perhaps twelve stood on the steps. The child was shabbily dressed and had a mop of shaggy blond hair and the saddest blue eyes Rupert had ever seen. They stared up at him with an anxious expression.

"Uncle Holmes?" the boy asked.

Rupert Snodgrass glared down at him, unable to process the question. His sleep-addled brain couldn't imagine who the boy was or what he was doing on his doorstep. *"Uncle?"* Did the boy say, *"Holmes"*? Well, he certainly wanted nothing to do with any children, especially a child related to Sherlock Holmes.

Without a word, Snodgrass slammed the door shut and wandered back to bed. But his head had barely touched the pillow when the knocking began once more. Whoever this rascal was, Snodgrass thought, he evidently had no idea of the danger he was putting himself in.

This time Rupert Snodgrass practically tore the door from its hinges.

"What?" he demanded. He was furious.

"My name is Griffin Sharpe. I'm looking for my uncle, Sherlock Holmes. I thought he lived at this address."

"You're wrong. He lives next door."

Griffin stared at the man, looking confused. "Then this isn't 221 Baker Street?"

"It is. But Sherlock Holmes lives at B, and I live at A. *He* is upstairs, and if you're looking for *him*, then you've come to the wrong place. Stop bothering me."

Griffin was about to turn away when something caught his attention. It was the distinctive color of the man's eyes. They weren't quite blue and not quite green, and their size and shape reminded him of someone else's, someone he knew very well . . .

Mother's eyes!

Griffin's heart sank as his eyes darted over the man, taking in the tiniest details. Now that he looked, he could see several family resemblances. In addition to the eyes, his uncle's hands, his jawline, and the color of his hair told him everything he needed to know. It was hard to accept, but the visual evidence suggested that this horrible man was his uncle!

Griffin stared up at the slovenly figure in the doorway and frowned. The man looked like he hadn't slept in weeks, and Griffin was pretty certain the smell of cheese that wafted toward him wasn't cheddar. But there was one last question he needed to ask to be sure. He hoped that somehow, his observations had been wrong.

"Um . . . sir, can I ask one other question? Does the name 'Snoops' mean anything to you?"

"W-what? Snoops? Where did you hear that?" Snodgrass blustered. "Who told you that name?"

"Never mind," the boy said meekly. His eyes hadn't deceived him. The great Sherlock Holmes was not his uncle after all.

"I, er, see that your real name is Robert Snodgrass. I'm sorry; I should have noticed it sooner," Griffin said.

Snodgrass looked startled and then annoyed. After a moment, he said, "What, is that some kind of magic trick? How did you figure that out?"

"I simply noticed the initial R monogrammed on your dressing gown pocket. Robert is the most popular name that begins with that letter. And when I glimpsed the Snodgrass coat of arms hanging in your parlor, I figured that it must be your last name."

Observant. Snodgrass realized that the boy had determined all of this after his having had the door open for only a few moments. But he was tired and hungry, and he wasn't in the mood to be lectured in the fine art of observation by some arrogant child.

"Well, you're wrong. My name's Rupert, not Robert. And just who do you think you are, boy? I don't have time to stand here arguing with you. I'm a very busy man!" he said.

A look of regret flickered across the boy's face. "I-I'm sorry. I assumed that I wouldn't be an intrusion, being that we're family."

"Family?" Rupert Snodgrass barked. He gave the boy a ferocious stare. "I don't have any family. I thought you said Holmes was your family."

In answer, the boy reached into his pocket and removed a small envelope. Snodgrass snatched it from his outstretched hand.

The detective's eyes darted over the paper, taking in the contents. It was from the same address as a letter he'd received weeks earlier. He hadn't bothered to open the first letter, because he had mistakenly assumed it was from a bill collector.

Rupert tore open the envelope and found that it contained some money and a note from his sister who lived in America. After a moment he realized, to his horror, that the letter's intention was to introduce him to his nephew. His sister had sent the boy to stay with him for the entire summer because she said it "would be a valuable cultural and character-building experience for Griffin to learn about my homeland."

Character building experience? Obviously his sister, whom he hadn't spoken to in years, had underestimated her brother's aversion to children. As far as Rupert Snodgrass was concerned, he would rather forget that he had ever been a child himself.

As if reading his uncle's mind, Griffin Sharpe turned and gave his uncle an awkward smile.

"I'm looking forward to getting to know you, Uncle," the boy said quietly. And then, indicating his suitcase, he added, "I hope I won't be a bother."

A BAD START

So now, after traveling thousands of miles to London and being shown to a very shabby room that smelled of mothballs and mildew, Griffin felt a surge of regret. He realized that by blurting out the connection between the initial on his uncle's dressing gown and the painting of the Snodgrass coat of arms in the hallway, he must have made his uncle feel stupid. Like so many times before, he'd said his thoughts as soon as they'd popped into his head. And it didn't take a genius to notice that the minute he'd mentioned it, his uncle had thought him annoying and rude.

Griffin assumed that his Uncle Rupert would probably send him home on the next boat to Boston. And if he didn't, it was most likely going to be a very long and painful summer. He'd have to do his best to bother his uncle as little possible, to be as quiet as a mouse, and to never, under any circumstances, try to act "clever." He sighed. As usual, he'd ruined his chances at making a friend because he couldn't keep his mouth shut.

Griffin began unpacking his suitcase for lack of anything

else to do. A few hours earlier it had looked very much like he was going to be the nephew of the great detective he'd read about on the train. But now, here he was, alone in London with an uncle who was about as unlike Sherlock Holmes as he could possibly imagine. Griffin's fleeting hope of finding someone who understood him and would be happy to have him around had disappeared.

After placing his things in the shabby wardrobe, he sat on the edge of the bed and stared out the window. Although it was late, he could still hear the sounds of carriages rolling up and down the cobblestone streets. He was homesick. He had never wanted to see his mother and father more in his entire life.

Griffin's stomach grumbled. He couldn't remember the last time he'd eaten. When he'd been living in the fantasy that had included being the nephew of a great and successful detective, he'd assumed he would be welcomed with a magnificent tea served by Mr. Holmes's landlady, Mrs. Hudson. The stories in the magazine had described her cooking so well that his mouth had watered.

So much for that idea, he thought. Although Mrs. Hudson owned both apartments, apparently she didn't provide the same services for each of her tenants. Judging by the way he'd been welcomed, Griffin assumed that it was probably because Sherlock Holmes was nicer than his uncle was.

Griffin's hand strayed to his pocket. He had a little bit of spending money. If he had only known what was in store for him, he would have stopped at one of the vendors on the street he'd passed on his way to his uncle's apartment. But at the time he'd been so eager to meet him, he had rushed by all of the pie sellers and chestnut roasters without a backward glance.

Thinking back, he remembered one of the pastry shops he'd noticed on Baker Street. His quick eye had seen, even in passing, that it had been stocked with several varieties of pastry he'd never seen before, but all of which had looked delicious.

He pictured the blue sign with gold letters. He could clearly read the name, *Mrs. Tottingham's*, painted on the window with the *s* on the end of the name having a small chip out of the corner. There had been a woman inside dressed in a black-and-white striped dress, whose apron was covered with white dust . . . flour, Griffin assumed. She had a small mole on her left earlobe, bottle-green eyes, a lovely smile, and plump, rosy cheeks. He'd always heard the phrase "Never trust a skinny baker," and thus concluded that the treats in this shop would be particularly tasty. Sweets had always been rare at the Sharpe home because of his father's meager salary, but Griffin thought that just this once it would be worth spending a little of his money on something delicious.

The thought of all those lovely pastries sitting uneaten in the bakery window made his stomach growl even more loudly. One of the downsides to having a photographic memory was that the images in his mind were so real, it almost felt like he was right there, staring through the shop window.

Griffin pushed his hands firmly against his growling stomach and made a mental note to visit the bakery tomorrow. He would go first thing in the morning, providing his uncle didn't take him to the train station to send him back to Boston.

He'd barely had this depressing thought when his uncle's

voice floated down the hall, calling, in a not-very-nice-way, "Boy! Get down here!"

And Griffin, letting out a long sigh, assumed by the tone that it probably wasn't to call him downstairs for dinner.

THE SNODGRASS RULES

When Griffin felt nervous, he counted things. Counting helped him restore order to his troubled inner universe. Even though there were things that he couldn't control, numbers were a constant. They never changed and, when added together, they created an answer that was true.

And truth gave him comfort.

At school, he'd counted the nails in the classroom floor when the substitute teacher had unjustly accused him of cheating on his history exam because he'd answered every question correctly. Later that day he'd counted the spots of ink on the headmaster's desk when he'd been sent to his office for fighting. Even though Griffin hadn't thrown the first punch and was the one who ended up with a black eye.

And now, as he walked down the hall of his uncle's apartment, Griffin not only counted the number of floorboards (eighty-three), but also the number of flowers patterned on the carpet runner (one hundred thirty-six). But even with all those numbers rattling around in his head, he couldn't calm himself down. He could tell by the tone of his uncle's voice that he was in trouble for something, but he had no idea how he could have already offended him. After all, he'd barely unpacked! What could he have possibly done in so short a time? It didn't make sense. And things that didn't make sense made Griffin feel very uncomfortable.

Upon entering the parlor he saw his uncle slouching in front of the blackened fireplace, staring down into the empty grate. Griffin scanned the room and was surprised to see that this did not look like any parlor he had ever seen before. Magnificent-looking gadgets, all in various stages of assembly or repair, were piled high upon every available surface, and the walls were covered with weapons. Griffin counted fifteen futuristic-looking brass pistols, seven long rifles with elaborate brass scopes and clockwork sights, three strange looking helmets with goggles of green glass, two armored vests, and the stuffed head of some exotic animal that looked as if it had come from another world entirely.

Gazing around the parlor, he noticed that on the bookcase were several polished, wooden boxes, each with a glowing gray glass panel on one side. Next to the sofa was something that reminded Griffin of an Edison phonograph, but instead of a turntable, it had a wheeled cabinet positioned beneath its large, conical horn. And piled in every corner were pulleys, ropes, gears, rods, switches, wires, domes, hinges, and wheels.

Griffin wanted to examine all the objects to figure out what they were and how they worked, but his uncle's stern gaze stopped him before he touched anything. Old newspapers and moldy teacups were stacked on every space not occupied by mechanical things, and Griffin had to work his way carefully through the room, hoping that he wouldn't accidentally break anything.

"Sit," Rupert commanded. And Griffin, seeing no other spot, cleared away a rusty oilcan and promptly sat down upon the floor. His uncle glared at him, snatched up the oilcan as if it were made of gold, and set it gently atop a pile of other cans. However, as soon as his uncle let go, the entire tower of cans toppled to the floor with a crash.

Snodgrass sprang into action, chasing down the cans as they rolled in every direction. He tried awkwardly to snatch one of them before it rolled underneath the sofa and slipped, landing unceremoniously on his rump.

Griffin bit his lip, trying hard not to laugh. His uncle attempted to get up gracefully, but as he did, he knocked over a bin filled with nuts and bolts. The parts flew into the air and ricocheted off of the ceiling, showering down upon him.

As the last of the nuts and bolts hit the ground, Snodgrass straightened his tie and cleared his throat, trying desperately to look dignified. But his hair was messy, and he looked so frazzled that Griffin could barely contain his laughter. Snodgrass sniffed and, after brushing imaginary flecks off of his rumpled suit, said in a pompous voice, "You have disrupted my work, young man."

"Sir?"

"My work. This!" Snodgrass made an irritated gesture at the many gadgets. "Your very presence in my house jeopardizes *everything*."

"I'm afraid I don't understand, sir," said Griffin.

"This is my working room, and you—have—disrupted

—my—ability—to—concentrate," his uncle stated, biting off each word.

Snodgrass's face had grown increasingly red and blotchy as he spoke. A large vein pulsed on his forehead and tiny beads of sweat gleamed on his forehead, making his damp, unshaven face shine like a polished apple.

Griffin squirmed uncomfortably.

"I'm a very busy man and have no time for children. Sending you here without any advance warning was presumptuous and rude. My sister and I haven't spoken in years!"

Griffin had to hold his tongue to keep from reminding his uncle that his mother had sent several letters to him about the situation.

Snodgrass spat into the empty fireplace. "However, the fact that I am living on limited resources makes it difficult to refuse the money she sent. In order to make this situation work for us both, you will have to obey my rules."

Griffin was quite sure the rules wouldn't be easy to follow.

"Rule number one: you are not allowed, under any circumstances, to enter this room. This is my private workspace where I do my most important thinking. The devices displayed around you have been designed to help me solve crimes. Important cases vital to the safety and security of the British Empire depend on my ingenuity. In other words, this is a place where children do not belong."

"Oh, are you an Enquiry Agent?" Griffin blurted out in excitement. "Is that what these devices are for . . . detective work?" Once again he'd been unable to resist the urge to ask a question and, after the words had left his mouth, he winced. When would he learn to control his tongue?

His uncle stared at him, his lips twitching with anger. After a visible struggle, he answered his nephew's question.

"Yes," his uncle said. "I am a private *investigator*."

"I see. Just like Mr. Holmes next door! How wonderful!" Griffin exclaimed.

"I am nothing like Mr. Holmes!" Snodgrass barked. "My machines provide a far more practical method for solving crimes than his so-called 'deductive reasoning.'"

Snodgrass paced in front of the fireplace, growing more agitated. "I haven't had a client in weeks! Everyone automatically assumes that he is the greatest detective in London, but they're wrong! My neighbor is nothing more than an arrogant, self-important, pompous . . . ," he spluttered, trying to find words. He finally continued with, "Do not ever mention his name to me again! Do you understand?"

Surprised by his uncle's reaction, Griffin didn't know what to say. "Understood," he replied hesitantly.

"Right," said his uncle sternly.

Snodgrass pushed a lock of his thinning hair back on his scalp and gathered his composure. "Now, let's get down to business. Rule number two: you are to stay out of my way. I don't want to see, hear, or smell you, understand? You are to leave the house every day by eight o'clock in the morning. You may return for dinner at six o'clock. Do I make myself clear?"

Griffin nodded. Two very harsh rules. The first was understandable, but the second . . . He felt angry and struggled to control his temper. He couldn't believe his uncle would force him out onto the streets every day. It was no way to treat family!

"Now then," his uncle continued in a tight voice, "if we

keep out of each other's way, I'm sure we can get through this summer with as little conflict as possible. Those are my rules. You're dismissed."

Griffin took a deep breath and fought the urge to tell his uncle how unfair he was being. Instead, he decided to turn the other cheek and be polite. "May I ask one more thing?"

Griffin's uncle gave him a withering stare. "What is it?"

Griffin had been about to ask whether or not he was allowed something to eat when the question froze in his throat. Someone . . . *something* had entered the room. It walked like a man, but was made entirely of brass. It was about the same height as Griffin, but it had a brass handlebar mustache and glowing blue eyes. As it walked it gave off tiny puffs of steam, and Griffin could hear the sound of gears clicking as it made its way into the center of the room.

It was so much better than anything Griffin had ever imagined.

"A mechanical man!" he said.

Uncle Snodgrass sniffed. "A mechanical *butler*. One of my more ingenious devices."

Griffin stared at the robotic man, overcome with awe. The butler turned toward Griffin and bowed ever so slightly.

"Would Master require anything this evening? A pot of tea, perhaps?" the butler said in an electronic voice.

"Not necessary, Watts. You may retire to your quarters."

With a respectful nod, the robot turned and marched slowly out of the room. Griffin felt hopeful again. Maybe the summer wouldn't be so bad after all. The butler was surely able to play games. Maybe he could even take the butler on outings for company. No one back home would ever believe it! But then his uncle's raspy voice yanked him out of his daydream and back to reality.

"And one more rule: you're to have no contact with Watts. He only obeys my orders, understand? Now, off with you."

Griffin couldn't believe how unfair it all was. He couldn't think of anything polite to say, so, blinking back tears, he stood, bowed, and strode from the room as quickly as possible without running. When he returned to his small room, he shut the door quietly behind him with as much dignity as he could muster.

What had he ever done to deserve such treatment? It wasn't his fault his uncle hadn't read and responded to his mother's letters. All of his uncle's rules were frustrating and disappointing, but the rule about Watts just seemed cruel. If his uncle weren't interested in spending time with him, he could at least let Griffin play with the butler so he didn't have to be alone all the time.

He sniffed and ran his sleeve quickly across his eyes. *I'm not going to let him get to me*, he thought. *I have to be strong.*

Then, not knowing what else to do, he got ready for bed, all the while grumbling to himself. Not that it did him any good. He just couldn't understand why his uncle seemed to hate him. Griffin had been so excited to come to London. And everything he had seen so far that his uncle had created was truly amazing. He would have loved to learn from him. But instead it looked like he was on his own, as usual. Griffin turned down the gas lamp and crawled beneath the thin quilt. He felt terribly lonely. He didn't want to cry. He was, after all, almost thirteen years old. But the situation with his uncle, his hungry stomach, and the disappointment of having to spend an entire summer away from his family was almost too much.

I wonder what Mother and Father are doing right now. Griffin thought wistfully. He pictured the parsonage with its little stone fireplace. Father would be reading the Bible next to the crackling logs and his mother would be making supper. Maybe she'd be cooking chicken and dumplings, his favorite meal.

Griffin took a deep, shaky breath and willed himself to be strong. Giving in to feeling homesick would only make things worse. After murmuring a prayer, making sure to express his gratefulness for those things he had to be thankful for and trying not to just complain to God about those things he couldn't control, he closed his eyes.

He was more tired than he realized. And just as he was about to drift off to sleep, sweet music drifted down from up above. He was vaguely aware of a violin playing overhead, and its mournful sound soothed his troubled heart. As the boy slowly drifted into unconsciousness, he automatically counted the muffled notes, the time signature of each one, and exactly how many bow strokes were needed to produce each phrase on the musical staff.

And little did he know that as he played his violin, Sherlock Holmes, his uncle's upstairs neighbor, was doing exactly the same thing.

SUNDAY

It was a beautiful June morning. The sun shone down on the cobblestone streets, making the damp stones glitter like diamonds. Griffin, who had been up before dawn, stared down at the empty shopkeepers' windows and neatly painted signboards. He could see no street vendors setting up their wares or chatting with the other early risers.

For a moment, he thought perhaps people in England didn't get up as early as folks in America. Then he realized that it was Sunday morning, the day of rest. Shops were closed, and anybody not attending church would probably be at home, sleeping in. Unfortunately for his growling stomach, that also meant there would be no chance to visit the bakery he'd passed the previous evening.

But the day was cheery enough. It seemed impossible for anyone to be gloomy on such a wondrous summer morning. *Except for Uncle Snodgrass*, he thought. Griffin felt reasonably certain that it would take much more than a pretty day to warm up his uncle.

Griffin washed and dressed and then walked down the

hall, hoping for breakfast. He found his uncle, wearing a frayed blue dressing gown, seated at a small table reading the morning paper. Griffin automatically counted the number of threads hanging from the sleeves of his uncle's robe (eleven on the left, three on the right). And he also noticed that Rupert's hair was sticking up in all directions, which meant that his uncle clearly had no intention of going to church.

"Good morning, Uncle," Griffin said.

After getting no response, Griffin continued, saying, "It's Sunday, Uncle Rupert, and I was wondering, would you like to attend services with me? I'm unfamiliar with the churches in the area and was hoping to find a Methodist chapel."

Snodgrass grunted and turned the page of his *London Times*. "Dinner will be at six o'clock. If you are late, I won't wait for you."

Griffin nodded, sighed, and strode from the kitchen. He walked out the front door and made sure that he was careful to close it quietly behind him. *Well, that didn't go very well.* Griffin decided to pray while he was at church that he and his uncle could find a way to get along.

Outside, Griffin signaled to one of the shiny, black hansom cabs rolling up and down Baker Street. He'd never hailed his own cab before, but had seen his father do it many times. It wasn't long before one of the cab drivers saw his outstretched hand and stopped at his uncle's stoop. The cab was pulled by a black horse with a white spot on its rump. The friendly-looking cabman smiled down at him, surprised someone so young was looking for a ride.

"What can I do for you, son?"

"I'm new to London," Griffin said. "Would you mind taking me to the nearest Methodist church?"

"Hmmm, you'll be wanting the Wesley Chapel," the cabman answered. "It's a bit of a ride though."

The cabman looked down at Griffin with a doubtful expression. Griffin immediately withdrew a little of the pocket money his parents had provided for his trip.

"Will this do?" he asked.

The driver smiled and motioned away the coins. "It will, but you don't have to pay me until we get there. Hop aboard, lad."

Griffin climbed up into the carriage. His quick eye noticed that the leather seats were well cared for, that they'd been rubbed with saddle soap and some kind of special oil. They were very soft. Griffin also noticed that the interior was spotless, and careful repairs had been made where age or wear had cracked the mahogany wood inside the cabin.

But looking down, Griffin noticed a couple of tattered bits of red paper littering the cab floor. Assuming that the last passenger had left them behind, Griffin pocketed the scraps. The driver clearly took very good care of the carriage, and Griffin wanted to help keep the man's cab clean.

The hansom cab wound its way down the cobblestone streets at a brisk trot and, as they bounced along, Griffin felt himself relax. He was enjoying watching the city pass by and looking forward to church. He had never attended services at any church other than his father's, and he was interested to see what the differences were.

He was so distracted by the scenery that he was unprepared when the horse suddenly gave a terrified whinny and the cab screeched to a halt. Griffin was thrown forward into the seat opposite him, and his elbow smashed against the door.

Outside the cab, he heard a woman shriek. The sound sent chills up and down his spine. Trying to ignore the throbbing pain in his arm, Griffin opened the hansom cab's door. When he peeked outside, he was shocked by what he saw.

THE WOMAN, THE CLOCK, AND THE MONSTER

A terrified woman stood in front of the snorting, frightened horse. Griffin noticed right away that there was something wrong with her. She had a wild look on her face, her hair was disheveled, and he could tell that she'd dressed in a hurry, for her boots were not properly laced and one of her gloves was turned inside out.

"Oy! What're you trying to do, woman, kill somebody?" the cab driver shouted.

Seeing that the woman needed help, Griffin climbed down from the cab and rushed over to her side. "Can I help you, ma'am? Are you all right?" he asked.

Up close, Griffin could tell how disoriented and frightened she was. She had green eyes, three light wrinkles by her left eye and four on her right; her perfume, a light floral scent, was expensive, probably French; and her name was probably Sarah (a small locket around her neck bore the letter *S,* and Sarah was the most popular name that began with that letter). He also noticed that she was married. She had a ring on the third finger of her left hand, and she clearly did a considerable amount of sewing, judging by the small calluses on her otherwise delicate hands.

The woman looked up at him with a stricken expression. "I . . . I need to find a man named Sherlock Holmes, but I don't know who he is or how to find him. It's my husband . . . he's been . . ."

And just as these words were leaving her lips, the woman fainted. Griffin stared at her, completely confused. She was obviously in bad shape, and he wasn't entirely sure that she was in her right mind. Regardless, she needed help, so Griffin called up to the cab driver.

"Sir, could you help me take her back to Baker Street? I'd be happy to pay you whatever you require for the inconvenience."

The cab driver, who, in spite of losing his temper at the woman a few moments earlier, seemed to be a good sort of person, agreed quickly. Together, he and Griffin managed to help the unconscious woman into the cab, and soon they were racing back to the address Griffin had just left.

Griffin tried to make the woman as comfortable as possible, turning his jacket into a makeshift pillow. He'd never seen someone faint before, and if it weren't for the fact that he could see her pulse fluttering at her slim throat, he would have thought she had died. Because he was nervous, Griffin counted every address, every cab, and every person wearing a top hat on the way back to Baker Street. The woman lay motionless the entire journey, and her pale skin was clammy with sweat. He was very worried about her, and it made the trip seem twice as long.

When they finally arrived at 221 Baker Street, Griffin asked the driver to wait while he rushed up the stairs to Sherlock Holmes's apartment. His heart pounded as he knocked on Holmes's door, partly because of his fear for the woman in the carriage and partly because he was excited to meet the famous detective. But neither Sherlock Holmes nor Dr. Watson answered the door. Griffin waited anxiously, hoping that someone, even Mrs. Hudson, would appear, but nobody came.

What should I do?

He bit his pinky nail while he turned over every possible solution. He could take the woman to the police, but he had no idea how far away Scotland Yard was. Besides, she hadn't asked for police help. She was looking for a private detective. Maybe she didn't want to involve the police in whatever had happened to her husband.

There was only one decent solution. But Griffin couldn't help wondering how much trouble it would get him into. His uncle had made it very clear that he was not to come back home until dinner. Then again, this woman needed help and he couldn't abandon her. His uncle claimed to be a private detective. If he really were one, then it seemed right to notify him about her situation.

When the door to his uncle's apartment opened, Griffin was so nervous about how his uncle might respond to his breaking his rules that he could hardly find the words to speak. But after a moment he gathered his courage and told his uncle about the woman he'd met in the street and who was now lying unconscious in the hansom cab.

To Griffin's surprise, Snodgrass's curiosity seemed to be piqued. "She specifically asked for Sherlock Holmes?" he asked. "But didn't know where to find him or what he looked like?"

Griffin nodded.

A crafty expression flickered over Snodgrass's features. Then the scruffy man trotted down the steps toward the waiting carriage. "We mustn't leave the poor woman unattended," he called back to Griffin. "Tell Watts to brew some tea."

What? Evidently his uncle was throwing all of the rules out the window. Griffin couldn't be more pleased. His uncle might get a case, and he was able to get a closer look at the robot.

"Right away, Uncle!" Griffin called.

Dashing back inside the musty house, Griffin didn't have to look far to find the mechanical butler. He was in the entry, holding a strange cleaning device that made a sucking sound as he dragged it over the threadbare, Persian rug.

Griffin shouted over the loud roar of the machine. "WATTS, COULD YOU PLEASE MAKE SOME TEA?"

The robot didn't seem to hear him. It continued what it was doing, oblivious to Griffin's command. Griffin moved closer to a small, protruding button on the side of its head, something he assumed might be the robot's mechanical ear, and tried again.

"Tea! TEA!"

But once again, there was no response. At that moment, Griffin's uncle appeared, red faced and puffing, as he carried the unconscious woman up the stairs and into the entryway. As he made his way past his nephew and into the cluttered parlor, he called back to Griffin, "As I told you last night, he will only take orders from me. It will only work if you start every command with 'Rupert says.' Don't be stupid, boy."

Griffin was offended. He was anything but stupid. It wasn't fair to expect him to know how to do something that he had never been instructed how to do.

Turning back to the robot, he pronounced loudly, "RUPERT SAYS . . . MAKE TEA FOR THREE!"

At that command the mechanical man suddenly shuddered to a stop. Then it turned off the loud cleaning device, strode over to the kitchen, and began to brew a cup of Snodgrass's weak, watery tea.

Griffin smiled. The mechanical man was marvelous! As he watched Watts brew the tea and then pour it into three chipped cups, he heard a soft moan coming from the other room. Griffin hurried into the parlor, where he saw his uncle bent over the woman, massaging her hand.

"Where am I?" she asked in sleepy, disoriented voice.

"Somewhere safe," Snodgrass replied.

"Are . . . are you Mr. Holmes?" the woman asked.

Griffin was shocked to hear, instead of the usual, angry outburst at the mention of his nemesis's name, his uncle reply in a very sweet voice, "I'm at your service, madam."

He had avoided answering her question directly, but his uncle was clearly trying to trick the woman. He was allowing her to believe *he* was the great detective so that she would hire him. Griffin couldn't let his uncle lie to that poor woman. It just wasn't right.

"Ma'am, I think what my uncle is trying to say is that while he's not actually Sherlock Holmes, he is still able to help you with your case—," Griffin began. His uncle's glare cut him short. The woman was clearly confused, staring first at Griffin and then at his uncle. Then her expression grew frightened.

"What's going on? I demand to know where I've been taken and who you gentlemen are!"

For the first time since Griffin had seen her, the woman

seemed to have fully regained her faculties. Snodgrass fumbled while trying to search for an adequate explanation. Griffin stepped in.

"Ma'am, my name is Griffin Sharpe and this is my uncle, the brilliant inventor and crime expert Rupert Snodgrass. I happened upon you after you nearly injured yourself in a collision with the hansom cab I was riding in. Before you fainted, you mentioned that you wanted to speak with Sherlock Holmes, so I instructed the driver to take us to here, to 221 Baker Street."

Griffin hesitated before continuing. His uncle was staring at him with an unreadable expression. He knew he was on dangerous ground. But he felt that he must, no matter what the consequences, tell the truth. After taking a steadying breath, he continued, "Mr. Sherlock Holmes was not at home, and seeing no other option, I decided to alert my uncle, who is an expert in such matters, to your situation. He acted with immediate concern and brought you here, to the apartment next door."

The woman's eyes narrowed as she absorbed the information. Griffin was pleased to notice the fear was already gone. After glancing around the room at the inventions that occupied nearly every space, she seemed to accept Griffin's explanation of things.

"You mentioned that Mr. Snodgrass here is an expert on crime"—she turned to Griffin's uncle and gave him a serious look—"and seeing that my situation is desperate, I do not care whether he is Sherlock Holmes or not. All I need is help."

Griffin noticed a slight relaxing of his uncle's features at these words, evidently relieved that she was willing to overlook his lie. Clearly all that mattered now to his uncle was that he had a paying client. And especially that Sherlock Holmes was unable to get to her first.

The woman turned back to Griffin and spoke. "You seem like a trustworthy young man. What I have to say is quite extraordinary. Therefore I ask you to believe that what I am about to tell you is the absolute truth."

Clearly irritated that the woman was directing her conversation at Griffin, Snodgrass interjected. "Madam, if I could have your attention, please. Simply relay the details of what is troubling you and I assure you, I will do all I can to help. My, er, nephew is newly arrived from America and has no experience in these sorts of matters. He's just a boy." Griffin's uncle smiled in a condescending way, showing way too many teeth.

Griffin was happy to see that this did not have any effect on the woman in the least. She continued to focus her attention on Griffin. She cleared her throat, straightened her rumpled dress, and said, "My name is Sarah Dent. My husband, Frederick, is a clockmaker. Two nights ago, he told me that a client had asked him to meet him on a matter of special business. It was about a very special clock, so special, in fact, that his client refused to bring it to the shop—for fear of being followed. He insisted that they meet by the banks of the River Thames at six o'clock the following morning instead."

She hesitated, as if deciding whether or not to continue. Her expression changed, and Griffin thought she looked as if she might cry.

After waiting a moment, she said in a shaky voice, "Forgive me, but this next part is a bit difficult. All day I waited for my husband's return. As the hour grew late, I began to wonder what had happened. My husband, you see, is very punctual. He lives by his pocket watch and has never been home any later than seven thirty. But last night, he didn't come home at all."

Mrs. Dent sniffed and her eyes filled with tears. Griffin was thankful that he'd thought to place a clean handkerchief in his pocket that morning and offered it to her. The woman took it gratefully and, after giving him a watery smile, continued her story.

"I was up all night, feeling more terrified by the hour. And then, early this morning, I was surprised by the arrival of a strange visitor. He introduced himself as James Dunn, a local fisherman and member of something called the Angler's Club. He said that my husband was gone forever and that he had seen the entire thing happen. Truth be told, if the man hadn't seemed so genuinely frightened, I don't know that I could have believed what he told me."

"Pray, tell me what happened, Mrs. Dent," Snodgrass said, urging her along. "I'm sure I shall be able to bring the villains to justice." He gestured around the parlor at the assortment of steam-driven gadgetry. "I am equipped with technology capable of solving even the most difficult of mysteries."

"You don't understand, sir. According to Mr. Dunn, my husband wasn't kidnapped or murdered." She looked imploringly at Griffin and his uncle. Then, choking back a sob, she said, "My husband was eaten by the Loch Ness monster."

THE WATCHER

The hansom cab waited outside the Baker Street address for a long time after Griffin and his uncle had taken Mrs. Dent inside. The burly driver stroked his beard as he stared up at the illuminated window. Things weren't going according to plan.

His boss had instructed him to patrol Baker Street, and he'd been doing so for several hours before Griffin had flagged him down. He'd refused the countless offers of other passengers wanting a ride because he wasn't really a driver at all. His name was John McDuff. And he was one of the most wanted men in England.

Mr. Moriarty isn't going to like this, he thought.

He was supposed to be watching to see if Sherlock Holmes or Rupert Snodgrass had been alerted to their robbery. Pulling off that heist, one that had involved over two tons of explosives, had been a masterful feat. It was a theft only a couple of criminal geniuses like the Moriartys could have orchestrated.

The new Moriarty had devised a crane capable of

transporting the load, and then divided the explosives between hansom cabs that transported the stolen goods to a secret train station, right under the watchful eye of Scotland Yard! The plan was, in John McDuff's opinion, nothing less than inspired.

This new Moriarty is even more brilliant than his cousin, the Professor, McDuff thought. After all, hadn't he heard that the man possessed three degrees in engineering from Oxford and additional degrees in science from Harvard University in the States? With that kind of education, it had come as no surprise that the Professor had placed his younger cousin in charge of this caper. Everyone thought it was the best move the old man had made in years. But now, the careful plan made by the two cousins had encountered its first snag.

Everyone in the criminal underworld knew about Rupert Snodgrass and treated him like the amateur sleuth he was. There were many times that Snodgrass had been watched from the shadows as he struggled to put the clues to a mystery together. He was certainly no Sherlock Holmes, but he could still complicate things.

This boy, on the other hand, was something new. And McDuff didn't like what he'd seen so far.

He had picked up the boy hoping he would reveal something, but assumed it was a long shot since he was just a child. But he had reacted quickly to the hysterical woman and had taken charge of the situation in a very adult manner. However, what had truly alarmed him was that when he had turned around to check on the boy, he had seen Griffin pick up the tiny bits of paper on the floor of the cab and pocket them. He should have cleaned the cab more carefully after the transport to the river the night before. How could he have been so careless?

He considered not reporting what had happened, but he realized with a sinking feeling that the new Moriarty would already know. He had eyes and ears all over London.

And he wasn't the type to forgive any mistakes.

AN UNEASY ALLIANCE

The following morning, Griffin Sharpe and Rupert Snodgrass climbed inside a carriage sent by Mrs. Dent. It was a rainy Monday, the kind that is usually best spent warming one's toes in front of a roaring fire. But in spite of the foul weather, Griffin's spirits were not dampened. In fact, for the first time since arriving in England, he was having fun.

"I cannot understand why she insisted that you be a part of the investigation," Griffin's uncle said grumpily as he settled himself into the seat opposite Griffin. "I find the whole idea preposterous. This is no business for a child."

Snodgrass removed his tattered brown hat and shook it, scattering water all over the inside of the cab. Griffin noticed that the ragged bowler was stained in several places. The largest of the grease spots was from some kind of machine oil, and its mangled brim had fireplace ash and something that looked like the remains of scrambled eggs around its edge. Overall, it was the saddest excuse for a hat he'd ever seen.

"I think she trusts me," Griffin answered, smiling.

Rupert Snodgrass scowled. "Well, I don't want you making a nuisance of yourself, understand?"

"Yes, Uncle," Griffin said, careful to keep from looking as excited as he felt.

The fact that he was being included in the investigation made him feel like he was finally going to get a chance to put his talents to good use. And it was definitely going to be more fun than wandering around the streets of London alone each day.

After hearing her story, Griffin felt sure that whatever the fisherman had seen, it couldn't have really been the Loch Ness Monster. He'd heard about the legend of the great dinosaur-like beast while studying a book on Scottish folklore at school. God was an imaginative creator, so such a creature might exist, but he had serious doubts about it showing up in the River Thames. It just didn't make any sense. First of all, someone would have noticed such a large creature traveling all the way from Scotland. And second, why would the beast eat only one man and no one else on the banks?

Griffin let his mind work on these questions as the hansom cab jogged along Baker Street and, after a quick turn, went east down Oxford Street. Griffin carefully noted the location and name of each shop they passed, committing them to his photographic memory. Now that he was officially part of an investigation, he thought that gathering a thorough sense of his surroundings might prove valuable.

Spotting a pastry vendor, he was reminded again of how long it had been since he'd eaten. Glancing back at his uncle, he decided to hazard a request. "Uncle?"

Snodgrass winced in irritation. "Enough of this 'Uncle' business. I would rather you refer to me as Mr. Snodgrass, if you please."

Griffin sighed, then continued politely, "*Mr.* Snodgrass, would it be all right if we stopped to get something to eat." He quickly added, "I have my own money and would be more than happy to pay for it."

"That won't be necessary," Snodgrass replied. "I had Watts go to the market this morning with some of the money your mother sent. You'll find whatever sustenance you need in there."

Griffin's uncle nodded to a leather satchel on the seat next to him. Griffin understood this to mean that he could help himself. Oh, how his stomach rumbled! It felt like an age and a half since he'd eaten.

Unfortunately, when he unwrapped the sealed package inside his uncle's satchel, he was sorely disappointed. Instead of delicious pastries or cheese or fruit, there were a couple of dried herrings and some kind of black, lumpy sausage that looked horrible.

"Black pudding," his uncle said. "Blood sausage. It's made from the blood of cows. You mother always loved it, so I thought you might too."

Griffin felt his stomach lurch. How disgusting! If this were what his uncle ate, it was no wonder he was always so short-tempered. However, Griffin was so hungry he thought he may as well give the food a try. He picked up one of the small fish by its tail and tried nibbling at its undersides.

It was awful. But Griffin felt sure that as bad as it was, it had to be better than the black pudding. Somehow he just couldn't picture his mother enjoying that, no matter what his uncle said. He ate as much of the fish as he was able, trying to imagine it was something else. But even with a photographic memory, he couldn't force the image of a lovely sandwich of sliced chicken and cheese onto the greasy little fish.

Finishing his strange meal, Griffin placed what remained of the fish and the untouched black sausage back in the satchel. While he had been eating, his uncle had been reading a copy of the *London Times*. After closing the leather satchel, Griffin noticed a small article on the front page of the paper that read,

ROBBERY AT LIMEHOUSE DOCKS

Police investigate the disappearance of imports arriving from China. The *Shanghai Scorpion*, a ship recently arrived from Hong Kong, bore several items of value for induction into the British Museum, including several ancient vases and some precious works of art given to Her Majesty from the Emperor.

Police were relieved to discover the treasures untouched, but fifteen hundred kilograms of fireworks were reported missing. The circumstances around the disappearance remain a mystery. Police suspect that the fireworks robbery was carried out by eager celebrants of an upcoming Chinese holiday.

"Uncle, I mean, Mr. Snodgrass?"

"What is it?"

"Did you happen to read the article on the front page, the one about the robbery?"

His uncle peeled down an edge of the paper and gave him a withering stare. "Of course I did. I read every section of the *Times*," he replied coldly.

"Don't you think that it sounds oddly suspicious?"

"Nothing outside of the ordinary, I assure you," Snodgrass said, returning to his paper. "It is as the police said, probably a group of Chinese ruffians who are too poor to afford their own fireworks. I don't have time to meddle with such trifling affairs."

"But it *is* strange," Griffin said. "After all, the robbers stole only fireworks and left the most valuable contents untouched. If they had stolen the Emperor's treasure and sold it, they could have purchased as many fireworks as they wanted. Also, to steal over fifteen hundred kilograms of fireworks would require more than just a few people. Converting kilograms to pounds that would be . . ."

Griffin did some quick mental calculations. "Three thousand three hundred pounds. That's a lot of fireworks."

Rupert Snodgrass lowered his paper, and Griffin felt as though his uncle were seeing him truly for the first time. He thought for a moment that maybe he would concede that Griffin had a point; he seemed to be considering something. But then his countenance changed.

"It's probably not as important as you think," Snodgrass replied. Puffing out his chest, he said, "I have been a detective longer than you have been alive, boy. I may, out of necessity, have to bring you along on this investigation, but it does not mean that you are anything other than an observer. Please keep your opinions to yourself."

Griffin nodded absently, but he wasn't really listening to his uncle. His quick mind was already working its way around the new mystery. He knew he should be thinking about the Loch Ness monster case, but the fireworks burglary was just too curious.

How strange, he thought, *that a man attacked by a monster and a robbery that makes no sense happened so close together.*

It was today's paper, so Griffin assumed that the robbery might have been conducted as recently as yesterday. Was it possible that the two mysteries were related? If his uncle would really allow him to be a part of the investigation, Griffin was certain he could find out.

"Mr. Snodgrass?" Griffin said.

"What is it now?" his uncle replied in an irritated voice.

Knowing he needed to state his case very carefully, Griffin took a deep breath and launched into his argument. "I was thinking. Perhaps I could be kind of like . . . like your Dr. Watson." Griffin was careful not to include the name Holmes. "I could help you with your cases and be your assistant. I'm very interested in investigative work, and I'm sure I could learn a great deal from your extensive experience. Perhaps I was *sent* here to help you."

If his uncle heard him, Griffin couldn't tell. His face was hidden behind the paper. But after a long moment, Snodgrass spoke. "What do you mean by 'sent,' boy?"

Griffin fidgeted awkwardly, then said, "You know, sent. By God."

It was a long time before Griffin's uncle replied. When he did, it was with a tight, restrained voice. "I do not believe in gods, nor do I believe in destiny. All I believe in are hard facts and scientific evidence. Besides, the very idea of your being my assistant is completely out of the question. In my opinion, the only reason you were *sent* was because your mother wished to have the summer to herself. Nothing else."

"But what about love?"

"Pardon me?"

Griffin leaned forward in his seat. "Love, Uncle. How can you truly say that there isn't a God when love is in the world?"

Snodgrass snorted. "'Love,' as you put it, is nothing more than a survival instinct. There are leading academics who believe it is simply chemical stimuli within the brain. We 'love' so that we can get what we want. It has nothing to do with any deity. The sooner you realize that, the better you'll understand the world we live in."

The rest of the cab ride down to the River Thames continued in silence. Griffin was having a hard time liking, much less loving his uncle. Snodgrass was mean, selfish, arrogant, and inhospitable. But Griffin believed in God and the power of His love, even if his uncle didn't. So he decided that he would extend kindness and understanding toward his uncle rather than judge him too harshly. And he wouldn't give up praying that someday they could even become friends.

As they bounced along the rain-drenched streets, Griffin noticed that the clouds had parted and a bright ray of sunshine illuminated the road ahead. Gazing into the distance, he could see the great River Thames sparkling and hear the faint cries of birds. The more he thought about it, the more it didn't really matter to him if his uncle thought his ideas were ridiculous. Somehow, deep inside, the conviction that he had been sent there for a purpose was growing. And, believing that, Griffin felt like he could face anything.

THE ANGLER'S CLUB

The hansom cab pulled up next to a low, flat building positioned near the banks of the river. The words *Angler's Club, Members Only* were written in elegant script on a sign mounted over the doorway, but the *M* in "Members" had been painted slightly crooked. The building's gray paint was chipped, revealing that it had once been painted brown underneath, and Griffin noticed that cats had made their home in the cellar. He observed this last part because some kind person had left a saucer of milk by the cellar door.

He noticed all of this in the space of time it takes to draw a breath. But after that, when he *did* breathe, he noticed the absolutely horrible stench of rotting fish. While it was understandable that the club would be in a location near the best fishing, the smell of old haddock and rotten perch was so strong that Griffin gagged a little. He suddenly wished he hadn't insisted that Mrs. Dent keep his only handkerchief. At that moment he would have given anything to filter out the terrible smell.

Snodgrass, on the other hand, seemed not to notice. After unloading a couple of large, leather cases from the cab, the scruffy man took a huge breath of the outside air and claimed that it smelled delicious.

As he followed his uncle inside the weathered-looking entrance, Griffin thought about the greasy fish he'd had for breakfast and felt his stomach lurch uncomfortably. *Lord, give me strength, because I'm sure not going to get any from eating my uncle's horrible food*, he thought miserably.

The interior of the Angler's Club resembled something between a dilapidated fishing shack and a gentlemen's club. Fishing buoys and nets hung from the ceiling, and gray driftwood decorated the mahogany paneled walls. A strange mix of salty old fishermen and British navy officers mingled inside. Hearing snatches of conversations going on all around him, Griffin judged that all of them shared one thing in common: the love of the sea.

He was counting the number of feathers on an admiral's hat and had arrived at the number three thousand two hundred and forty-six when a voice sounded next to him. "May I be of assistance?"

The voice belonged to a man situated at a small desk. Glancing at him, Griffin noticed that the man's hair was red, that he was wearing a particular kind of coat only issued in the navy, and that he had a tiny tattoo of a sparrow on his left wrist, which signified that he'd sailed over five thousand nautical miles. He knew this last fact because his uncle in Boston had served in the navy and had a tattoo just like it.

But the thing that interested Griffin most was that the man's desk was covered with several intricately designed model ships. They were some of the most detailed miniatures Griffin had ever seen.

"Pardon me, but did you build those ships? They're absolutely amazing!" Griffin said, gesturing to the models.

The man grinned and answered, "Yes, it's a hobby of mine. Do you like them?"

Griffin nodded. But before he could speak again, his uncle interrupted and said sharply to the young man, "We don't have time for idle chat, my good man. We're on important business. Does someone named James Dunn frequent this establishment?"

The man's smile faded and was replaced with a sneer as he turned to address Rupert. "Maybe he does, maybe he doesn't. Who's asking?"

"That's none of your business," Snodgrass fired back. "Just take us to him, if you please. I haven't got all day."

Seeing that his uncle's condescending attitude wouldn't get them very far, Griffin decided to try a different approach. "I'll bet those ships took months to complete. Would it be okay if I took a closer look?" he asked.

The young man's glare softened as he turned from Snodgrass to Griffin. "Go ahead, if you'd like," he said.

"Thanks."

Griffin took time to carefully study the different ships the man was building. Up close, he saw that they were even more wonderfully detailed than he had first thought. There was a beautifully painted tugboat with carefully constructed wooden decks, a clipper ship that had miniature figurines placed upon it, and, most wonderful of all, a magnificent ship that had been constructed inside of a glass bottle that had a lovely mermaid as a figurehead.

"Splendid!" Griffin gushed. "That mermaid's face is hardly

bigger than a match head. How on earth did you paint it so realistically?"

The young man beamed at the compliment. "The brush I use is very tiny. Her scales alone took me a year to paint," he said proudly. "And they're still not finished."

"I really like the detail."

The young man grinned and tousled Griffin's cap. "What did you say your name was?"

"I'm Griffin Sharpe and this is—," Griffin began, but Snodgrass interrupted.

"Rupert Snodgrass." Snodgrass flashed Griffin a forced smile, obviously making an effort to be more pleasant. "Yes, er, your miniature boats are, as the boy said, quite good." He cleared his throat and continued, "The reason we're here is because we were told that this was the best place in England to get some fishing advice and that Mr. Dunn was the man to speak to. Could you take us to him?"

Griffin could see right through the half-truth. His uncle was making an attempt to be a little friendlier, but he was still lying to the nice young man. However, before Griffin could point out the truth of the situation to the man, that they weren't really there to go fishing, the man had ushered them both to a small table in the back corner of the room.

When they arrived at the table, the grizzled old man who sat there nursing a mug of strong English cider gave them a suspicious glare.

"Mr. Dunn, I presume?" Snodgrass said, offering his hand. The old fisherman received it and shook it gravely.

"At your service. And who are ye?" he asked in a light, Scottish accent.

"Rupert Snodgrass, a private investigator. I've been sent to talk to you on behalf of Mrs. Frederick Dent. Can you spare a moment?"

Griffin noticed that the man looked very tired, like he hadn't slept for a couple of days. He hesitated before answering.

"What has she told ye?" Dunn asked.

"About the strange circumstances surrounding the disappearance of her husband. If you don't mind, I'd like to ask you a few questions."

Griffin thought that the man looked as if he didn't really want to talk to them, but he gave a short nod anyway and gestured to a couple of chairs. As Griffin sat down, he noticed that his uncle was rummaging through one of the large leather satchels he'd brought with him. After a moment, Snodgrass removed a strange-looking device and set it down on the table with a loud *clunk*.

It was a large black box. Griffin noticed several switches positioned on top of it and two small doors on its sides. Dunn eyed the machine apprehensively as Snodgrass opened the two little side doors and uncoiled two long cables with metal handles from inside the machine.

"Now, if I could just trouble you to hold the ends of these in either hand, we can begin," Snodgrass said.

Dunn looked apprehensively at the cables. "What for?"

"It is an invention of mine. I call it the Snodgrass Falsehood Detector. It will detect any, ah, inaccuracies in your description of the events you witnessed," he said.

James Dunn rose from his chair, his face flushed with anger. "Are you calling me a liar?" he growled. They were already off to a rocky start, thanks to his uncle's rude behavior.

Griffin acted quickly to try to calm things down. He knew they would never get anything out of the fisherman if he were angry.

"I'm sure that what Mr. Snodgrass means is that there is no reason to doubt your story. Using this machine is strictly a formality, isn't that right, Uncle?"

Snodgrass, surely seeing the dangerous glint in the fisherman's eye, quickly agreed. Mr. Dunn seemed mollified by Griffin's explanation and, after a little more persuasion from Griffin, held on to the ends of the Falsehood Detector cables.

"There we are. That's splendid," said Snodgrass as he turned the switches on the black box. Griffin heard a deep thrumming vibration begin to emanate from the machine, and a faint smell of ozone filled the air around them.

"Now then, we are almost ready," said Snodgrass as he switched his regular derby for an unusual hunting cap he'd pulled out with the machine. Griffin noticed that dangling from its earflaps were two wires that trailed down and plugged into the base of the machine.

"You may begin your account of what happened whenever you're ready, sir," Snodgrass instructed.

Dunn hesitated, glancing down at the two cables that he held in either palm. Griffin wondered if they were uncomfortable to hold. He hoped that his uncle was as good an inventor as he appeared to be, because if something went wrong and Mr. Dunn were injured as a result of the investigation, things could get pretty ugly.

"Right. Well, I was fishing at my usual spot on the Victoria Embankment. The fish weren't biting, so I decided to change locations. Mr. Dent, bless his soul, was standing by the edge of the water. I have visited his shop many times for repairs to my pocket watch and considered him a friend."

Snodgrass was listening with rapt attention, his hands holding the flaps of his cap close to his ears. He gestured for the man to continue.

"It looked to me as if he were waiting for somebody. I was about to call out and greet him, when suddenly the water began to bubble." Dunn grew more animated. Griffin listened, fascinated.

"The thing that came out of the water was at least seventy meters tall. And that was just the neck. Its head was enormous, as big as a small fishing boat!"

The fisherman's eyes grew wide. "I recognized it immediately. It was Nessie, the great beast from Loch Ness. A bad omen indeed. I do not know what she was doing so far from Scotland. But I tell ye, gentlemen, the mere sight of the monster took all the strength from me bones. I was too scared to do anything except stare. By the time I started moving again, well, poor Mr. Dent—"

The fisherman broke off, his voice cracking. After a moment, he continued,

"The beast swallowed him whole. One minute Mr. Dent was there on the shore, and the next"—he swatted his hand through the air for emphasis—"gone, he was. Then it weren't but two seconds later that I heard gunshots. Whether someone was firing at me or at the beast, I didn't know. I ran as fast as I could from the shore to get help. But, shameful as it is for me to admit, I didn't know who to talk to, about what I'd seen. The police would have thought me mad and anyone else, well, fishermen are well known for exaggerating their stories."

He took a deep drink from his cider mug and, after finishing, wiped a gnarled hand across his bushy, white mustache. "After a sleepless night, I decided to go see Mrs. Dent and tell her the terrible news," he said, then quickly added, "That's my story, gentlemen, and I stand by it."

The old fisherman glared down at the Falsehood Detector as if defying it to find any inaccuracy in his story. Snodgrass switched off the machine and nodded. Griffin wondered just how the machine worked and what his uncle had been able to hear through the modified earflaps of his cap. Snodgrass seemed satisfied with whatever the fisherman had told him.

He removed the strange cap and, replacing his moldy bowler on top of his head, said, "Thank you, Mr. Dunn. Now, if you don't mind, could you lead me to the exact location where the event happened?"

THE SCENE OF THE CRIME

Minutes later Griffin and his uncle were striding along the shore where James Dunn had indicated the attack had taken place. Luckily, the air was crisper and didn't smell as fishy as it had near the Angler's Club.

The boy's mind was buzzing with unanswered questions. The fisherman had seemed to be telling the truth. He'd noticed none of the little details in his manner that might have pointed to his lying.

"This is the spot," Snodgrass said.

Griffin stared down at the muddy bank. A deep trough was in the dirt, leading from the water's edge into the river. It looked as if it had been left by something extraordinarily large and heavy.

"I don't think Mr. Dunn was lying," Griffin said. "He didn't display any of the mannerisms most people use when they're not telling the truth."

"Such as?" Snodgrass said.

"Well, I've noticed that when people are lying they're usually reluctant to make eye contact, the pitch of their voice changes, and they act restlessly. Often their stories are filled with inconsistent details. It didn't seem to me that Mr. Dunn did any of those things."

Snodgrass snorted. "Deductive reasoning like that," he said, "is prone to speculation and error. I arrived at *my* conclusion by other, more scientific means."

Rupert puffed out his chest in a self-important gesture.

"The data I gathered showed that Dunn believes what he thinks he saw, whether it actually happened that way or not. You see, my Falsehood Detector measures a person's heart rate. When a person is lying, their pulse quickens. I am alerted to the change by an electronic tone that is conducted through the wires into the earflaps of my cap."

Snodgrass grew more excited as he described the workings of his invention. "Because his heart rate remained consistent, my machine detected no attempts at falsehood whatsoever. Those are the facts, boy, and *facts* don't lie. It's *elementary!*"

Griffin was impressed by the brilliance of his uncle's engineering ability. The man truly was a gifted inventor! But while they had each used different methods, he and his uncle *had* arrived at the same conclusion.

Even so, Griffin was able to admit that what his uncle had said about deductive reasoning had a lot of truth to it. Human observation did have limits, and sometimes observations could be wrong. There were people out there who, with practice, could hide their gestures when lying and fool the experts.

"You know, you have a point there, Uncle," Griffin admitted. "Perhaps a device like that should be implemented in more investigations. I'll bet your machine is something that the police would love to see. It could greatly improve the way cases are handled."

Belatedly, he realized that instead of calling him Mr. Snodgrass, he'd accidentally called him Uncle. Griffin winced, wondering if Snodgrass would reprimand him for the slip. But to his surprise, Snodgrass didn't correct him at all. Instead, Rupert Snodgrass seemed surprised and pleased by the compliment. "Yes, well. It might be worth considering at that," he said, sniffing with self-importance.

Griffin realized that Snodgrass was so absorbed in talking about the case that his attitude toward his nephew had thawed a little. Perhaps if they could stick to conversations about the investigation, they might actually get along.

Snodgrass removed one of the heavy bags he was carrying on his shoulder and began to rummage through it. Griffin looked down at the bank and examined the deep furrow in the earth that led to the water's edge. After studying it for a moment, he noticed something strange. Spaced evenly within the deep depression were several barlike tracks, each about twenty-five centimeters across.

Taking advantage of his uncle's distraction and willingness to talk, Griffin said, "There are tracks here, but they don't appear to be made by any kind of beast that I've ever seen. Perhaps they have been made by a machine. What do you think?"

"My thoughts exactly," replied his uncle. "But I'll know better after I measure the area for evidence."

Snodgrass, armed with a new device, walked over to his nephew's side. He was wearing green goggles and carried a long pole with an ornate metal bowl on the end of it. His uncle waved the bowl near the earth, back and forth in a sweeping movement just a few inches above the ground.

"What is it?" Griffin asked, indicating the device with a nod of his head.

"The Snodgrass Super Finder. It is a finely tuned instrument for locating and detecting hidden metal. The goggles I wear act as a filter, helping me to observe the slightest glint of reflected light off of metal surfaces."

Griffin smirked, resisting the urge to ask if everything his uncle had created contained the words *The Snodgrass* in the name. It seemed to Griffin that his uncle was very particular about getting credit for his work.

Snodgrass continued moving the large bowl back and forth over the unusual tracks. After a few moments, a small beeping noise sounded from the device. With a yelp of triumph, Snodgrass knelt and pawed around in the earth for a moment or two. Seconds later he drew an ornate pocket watch from the sand.

"Not exactly what I was looking for," he said, disappointed. "I was hoping to find some evidence of mechanics, perhaps a bolt or a discarded bit of wire. But I'm sure it's a clue nonetheless!"

Griffin moved closer to peer at the pocket watch. To his surprise, his uncle handed it to him. After studying it for a moment, Griffin noticed some words etched on the inside of the watch's cover.

To F, with all my love, S

It didn't take long for Griffin to deduce who "F" and "S" were. Frederick and Sarah Dent! He drew his uncle's attention to the inscription. Snodgrass brightened perceptively at the discovery.

"Well, that confirms that Frederick Dent was actually here. Good observation, boy."

Griffin felt quite proud upon hearing his uncle's praise. Glancing up, he could tell that Snodgrass was so completely preoccupied with studying the watch that he had probably delivered the compliment unconsciously. But to Griffin, it was one more small step on the road to friendship with his uncle.

"Thank you, Lord," Griffin prayed in a whisper.

"What's that?" Snodgrass asked, overhearing Griffin.

"Er, nothing," Griffin said, smiling, and turned back to examining the ruts on the muddy ground.

While his uncle scanned the beach with his contraption, Griffin walked along the shoreline, looking for more clues.

He didn't find anything of interest for several minutes until, about thirty feet from the shoreline, he spotted something strange. Kneeling down, he noticed several tiny scraps of red paper. They seemed familiar to him, but he couldn't think why. Then, in a flash, he remembered the scraps he'd found in the cab the day before.

Reaching into his jacket pocket, he removed the bits of paper and compared them to the ones in the dirt. They matched perfectly.

Griffin felt sure that there was some strange connection between the tracks on the shoreline, the paper on the shore, and the same unusual red paper he'd found in the cab. His heart beat with excitement as he considered the puzzle. After pocketing the paper, he turned his gaze to the rest of the shoreline. He walked around for several minutes, inspecting every bit of discarded fishing net, piece of glass, or anything else that might yield a clue. But he didn't find anything of interest.

The sun was starting to go down and the air was turning clammy. Griffin hunched up in his jacket and thrust his hands into his pockets.

"I guess that's all there is to see," he murmured. His fingers brushed the little scraps of paper in his pocket, and he turned over possibilities of what they might be in his mind.

Stationery? he wondered. But he dismissed the idea almost immediately. The texture of the paper was rough, and its red color would have made unusual material for correspondence.

He was about to turn back and go down to the shoreline where his uncle was scanning the beach when his attention was drawn to a group of nearby boulders. Several gulls were perched on the huge rocks, squawking loudly. But there was something that didn't look quite right. Griffin couldn't immediately place what it was, but then he noticed that there seemed to be something wrong with one of the birds. His expert gaze had picked it out from the group of others, noticing that it seemed unusually still.

Is it dead? he wondered.

Griffin walked over to the big stones, scattering all of the birds as he approached except for one. He reached out to touch it, and to his surprise he saw that it still didn't move. But it wasn't dead . . . It was something so cleverly designed that anyone not knowing about it would have thought it just one of the other birds.

Griffin lifted it up and found that it was unusually heavy. It was made of metal and painted so beautifully that even up close it looked like it was covered in real feathers. Looking closer, he saw that the eyes of the bird were made of clear glass. And as Griffin scrutinized them, he saw that they were actually tiny lenses.

He gasped. The thing was a camera! The most cleverly designed, smallest camera he'd ever seen!

"Uncle!" Griffin shouted.

Snodgrass's head jerked up when he heard Griffin's cry. Seconds later he was standing next to him, peering at the mechanical bird with an expression of awe.

"This is magnificent!" he said. "I've never seen the like . . ."

Snodgrass turned the bird over, and Griffin could see a tiny slot where photographic paper could be inserted between its metal feet. He also noticed that a pair of initials was etched into a metal plate right next to the slot.

"Who's N.M.?" he wondered aloud.

Snodgrass shrugged. "I don't know. Probably the inventor. But the more important question to ask is why was this put here? Someone wanted to take secret photographs of this area. I would bet my hat that whoever put it here had something to do with the disappearance of Frederick Dent."

Griffin glanced at his uncle's horrible bowler hat and grinned. Even though it was just a saying, he felt certain nobody would take his uncle's hat in any kind of bet.

"Should we take it with us?" Griffin asked, eyeing the amazing bird. Snodgrass pondered the question for a moment and then shook his head. "No, I don't think so. Whoever put it here will notice its absence." Snodgrass set the bird back down on the rock.

"Suffice it to say, we're dealing with a very sophisticated criminal mind. We must tread very carefully from now on."

He gestured at the bird. "Whoever created this might have many other such devices planted around London. We must be vigilant. He could be watching our every move."

As they walked back down the beach, Griffin's mind raced. Perhaps this was how it felt to be Sherlock Holmes when he was on a case. If so, Griffin could think of no greater thrill. Remembering a quote from the great detective in one of the stories he'd read in the *Strand Magazine*, he whispered it softly to himself, just to hear himself say the famous words.

The game's afoot!

THE PROFESSOR

I n a stately house in one of the most posh neighborhoods of London, an old man in a wheelchair stared out of an upstairs window. He stroked his unusually high forehead and gazed with sunken eyes down at the darkened streets, his mind ablaze with wicked ideas.

"Professor Moriarty, sir?" came a voice.

The professor pulled a lever on his steam-powered chair and swiveled around to face the newcomer. "What is it, Mr. Gordon?"

The shabbily dressed man removed a small envelope and handed it to Moriarty. "Someone's been tampering with camera 29. Your cousin insisted that I deliver the photographs to you immediately."

Moriarty opened the envelope with a yellowed fingernail. He removed the contents and held them up to the gaslight. The fuzzy image of a sad-eyed boy and a grizzled man wearing a tattered bowler were imprinted on the photographic paper. Moriarty's eyes glittered with recognition. He chuckled softly and handed the photos back to Mr. Gordon.

"Inform my young cousin that I am putting Mr. Snodgrass and his nephew on twenty-four-hour watch. I seriously doubt their capabilities, but it is always better to be safe than sorry."

Mr. Gordon nodded. "Should I inform Mr. Jackson?"

Moriarty considered for a moment and said, "Yes, Jackson would be perfect. But tell him that I expressly forbid violence at this stage. Doing so could draw unwanted attention."

Mr. Gordon bowed and exited the room. Moriarty swiveled his chair back to the window. He parted the elegant drapes with his clawlike hand. A few minutes passed before he saw a large, shadowy figure in a broad-brimmed hat exit from a nearby alley. The figure moved with animal-like agility down the street with his long cloak billowing behind him.

Moriarty smiled, observing Mr. Jackson as if he were a well-trained dog. He was confident there would be nothing that would escape his henchman's watchful gaze. Rupert Snodgrass was an amateur and would be easy to keep tabs on. His mental capacity was nowhere near the professor's supreme adversary, Sherlock Holmes, whose ability to anticipate his every move made his life so difficult.

Professor Moriarty felt reasonably certain that everything was still proceeding unobserved by Holmes and Snodgrass. When Holmes was on a case, the professor was usually alerted by one of his numerous spies and, so far, nothing seemed out of the ordinary. And when Snodgrass was on a case, well . . . he was usually foiled by his own lack of imagination. With the exception of the careless McDuff leaving those small scraps of paper in his cab, everything had progressed with utmost secrecy. He doubted that the boy—he had been told Griffin Sharpe was his name—would have the kind of experience to know how to draw any conclusions from such a seemingly trivial clue.

But sometimes, he had to admit, even amateurs got lucky. So if Snodgrass or his American nephew should accidentally stick their nose where it didn't belong, he would make sure that his dog Jackson was there to bite it off.

TEA AND SCONES

After a long day scanning the shoreline and finding no other clues of significance, Griffin and his uncle traveled by cab to Mrs. Dent's home. On the way, Snodgrass informed Griffin that she had specifically asked them to report their findings that afternoon over tea. Griffin had heard of English teatime and had always wanted to try it. His stomach was certainly more excited by tea at the Dents' home than anything they'd discovered by the shoreline that day.

Soon the cab pulled up to a stately section of London where some of its wealthier businessmen lived. Mrs. Dent's home was a lovely two-story building with a well-tended flower garden at its entry. They were greeted at the door by a young house-keeper. Griffin observed that the girl couldn't be more than two or three years older than he and was quite pretty. She smiled shyly at him as he and his uncle were shown inside to the parlor.

Griffin looked eagerly around the beautiful home and its elegant furnishings. He noticed the delicate, feminine touches that Mrs. Dent had placed throughout the house and was reminded of his mother. Pushing thoughts of home aside, Griffin focused on the delicious smells coming from what he guessed must be the kitchen.

As they entered the parlor, Mrs. Dent rose from the sofa and motioned for them to take the two chairs positioned near the fireplace. Although it was June, it was chilly in London, and Griffin was eager to warm up. He sat down, extending his hands toward the crackling flames. This was what he'd imagined it would be like when he'd read about Sherlock Holmes's apartment and Mrs. Hudson's hospitality!

The housekeeper appeared bearing a silver tray laden with a steaming pot of tea and several plates of small sandwiches, succulent-looking pies, and heaping piles of scones and cookies. Griffin's stomach growled loudly at the sight of so much food, and he blushed.

Mrs. Dent smiled. "Please help yourself, dear. You look like you haven't eaten a thing in weeks."

And Griffin realized that it wasn't that far from the truth. He had barely eaten anything since arriving in England. Seconds later Griffin was biting into a freshly baked scone covered with something Mrs. Dent called clotted cream. It tasted absolutely delicious. He was so preoccupied with eating that if it weren't for the fact that Mrs. Dent turned her attention back to the case, he might have forgotten about the entire investigation.

"Have you found anything yet?" she asked. "I'm absolutely beside myself with worry."

Griffin paused between sips of Earl Grey tea, noticing for the first time just how distraught Mrs. Dent was. He felt slightly ashamed that he'd not noticed her distress sooner.

"We're making headway," Snodgrass replied proudly. "With the help of my mechanical devices, we've been able to both authenticate the details of Mr. Dunn's story and the location of the actual event."

Mrs. Dent leaned forward, her eyes wide with anxiety. "Do you mean that everything he said was true? A monster actually ate my . . . my—"

Snodgrass interrupted. "Now, now, I don't believe that there is a monster or that anyone was *eaten*, Mrs. Dent. After conducting a thorough investigation of the shoreline, I believe that something else was at work, something mechanical. At this point, I'm suspecting that what we're dealing with might simply be a kidnapping."

"Kidnapping? But why would anyone abduct my husband?" she said.

"We have yet to establish a motive," said Snodgrass coolly. "But I'm convinced that with further investigation we shall."

Mrs. Dent began to breathe more heavily and quickly. And as Griffin watched, the color began to drain away from her face, leaving her pale and trembling. Griffin knew she was relieved that her husband had not been eaten, but kidnapping seemed to scare her almost as much. Snodgrass didn't seem at all aware of her condition as he helped himself to a small mince pie and another cup of tea before consulting his notes again.

Moved with compassion, Griffin went to sit next to Mrs. Dent and took her hand. "I'm truly sorry, Mrs. Dent," he said. "I'm sure what you're feeling right now is terrible. My uncle is very good at what he does. I've witnessed his amazing inventions at work, and they are truly remarkable. I promise you that we'll do all we possibly can to find him."

The woman looked up at Griffin with tear-filled eyes. She nodded and gave him a small smile as she tried to compose herself.

Snodgrass watched the two of them closely as he chewed. In all the years he'd been trying to build a reputation as a great detective, he'd never once truly thought about a client's feelings. A case was nothing more than a puzzle to be solved. Besides paying the bills, a new client mainly served as a chance for him to prove himself a superior investigator to Sherlock Holmes and make a name for himself, or at least that's what he had always thought.

But seeing the grateful look on Mrs. Dent's face gave him pause. For the first time, he saw her as she looked through Griffin's eyes. She was a person, not just as a client, and he could almost imagine the terror and anxiety she must be feeling at the loss of her husband.

He gazed at his nephew, wondering if he'd been judging the boy a bit too harshly. Although Griffin certainly possessed some of the same traits he despised in Sherlock Holmes, Snodgrass couldn't deny that there was something different about Griffin Sharpe.

Finally Mrs. Dent squeezed Griffin's hand and let it go, wiping the tears from her eyes and rising to show them out.

"Don't worry," Griffin assured her. "We will do everything we can to help."

Mrs. Dent pulled Griffin into a hug and called in her maid. She had the housekeeper pack a basket filled with the left-over pies and scones for tea so that they could "snack as they worked."

After a few moments of waiting, Griffin and Snodgrass climbed into a hansom cab and rolled away toward Baker Street. Griffin was staring out the window when his uncle cleared his throat to get his attention.

Snodgrass said, in a voice that was not unkind, "Do you remember what I said earlier about my set of rules?"

"Yes," answered Griffin.

"Well, I've changed my mind about a few of them."

THE PLAN

So it was with some surprise that Griffin found himself in his uncle's forbidden "working room" and was allowed to ask as many questions as he wanted. If Snodgrass had known what he was getting into, he might have thought twice, for Griffin had an inquisitive mind filled with questions. And, of course, he had an endless supply about the workings of his uncle's various gadgets and inventions.

"And what does that one do?" Griffin asked, pointing to one of the many futuristic pistols mounted on the wall.

"That is the Snodgrass Polysolar Transmogrifier," his uncle replied with a sigh. "It utilizes the sun's rays to produce a piercing beam of light, capable of destroying a target at over five hundred paces."

Griffin whistled. Could it be true? If the criminal underground mentioned in the Sherlock Holmes stories knew this stuff existed, he was sure they would waste no time in trying to steal every last item in the room.

"How come nobody knows what you've created in here?"

Griffin exclaimed. "Or do they?" He gave his uncle a questioning glance. Snodgrass looked uncomfortable.

"I have, er, had a few run-ins with the British government. Let's just say that they don't approve of what I'm doing." He gave his nephew a forced smile, but Griffin could see the anxiety beneath it.

"I see," Griffin said. "So I take it that if they found out about the weapons you have here, there could be trouble?"

"Of one sort or another, yes," Snodgrass grumbled. "That's why I'm swearing you to secrecy. Assuming that I can trust your rather overly obsessive need for absolute truthfulness, that is."

Griffin overlooked his uncle's somewhat insulting comment. Instead Griffin replied sincerely, "Of course you can, Uncle. I give you my word."

Griffin walked over to the bookcase, his attention now diverted by the boxes covered with switches and gray screens. "And what are these?" he asked.

Snodgrass brightened. "Ah, those. Well, I call those the Snodgrass Special Information Processors."

Snodgrass stood up and strode over next to Griffin. Lifting one of the wooden boxes from the shelf, he brought it to a cluttered tabletop. After moving several old teacups and a newspaper out of his way, he set it gently down and turned on a switch.

Griffin stared, unable to believe what he was seeing. Somewhere inside of the boxes, a steam engine whistled and puffed. Then the small, gray screen began to glow, and seconds later an elegant script appeared.

How may I be of service?

"What on earth?" Griffin whispered.

Snodgrass plugged the back of the box into a small type-writer. Then, turning to Griffin, he said, "Ask it any question you'd like."

Griffin stared up at his uncle in disbelief. "But how does it work?"

Snodgrass held up his hand and said, "It would be much too complicated to explain. But the most brilliant thing about its design is that it takes its information from every reliable news agency in the world by twenty-four-hour telegraph. It's usually fairly accurate."

Griffin stared down at the keyboard. He was reminded of the story of Aladdin and the genie, where the humble boy was given the chance to ask for three wishes. The funny thing was, now that he was able to ask the machine any question he wanted to, he couldn't think of a single thing to ask.

But then something that he'd been pondering entered his mind. Ever since the day before, when he'd seen the tracks on the shoreline, Griffin had formed an idea about what exactly might have kidnapped Frederick Dent. He typed his question, and seconds later an answer scrolled across the screen in the same elegant typeface.

"What have you got there?" Snodgrass asked, peering over his nephew's shoulder.

"I typed a question about submersibles," Griffin replied.

Now it was Rupert Snodgrass's turn to look confused. "I'm not sure what you mean," he said. "What are submersibles?"

Griffin turned excitedly to his uncle. "Ever since I saw the tracks leading to the river, I've been wondering if the thing that took Mr. Dent was some kind of submarine, a vehicle capable of traveling underwater. I read about them in a science journal back home. They can run both on steam and electric motors!"

Griffin's uncle looked thoughtful. He scratched at his scruffy beard and stared out the window.

"Hmm. I'm surprised I haven't thought of such a thing before. A Snodgrass Submersible Carriage. Pity. I could have done great things with such an idea . . ."

Griffin's uncle wore a faraway expression. Griffin interrupted his thoughts, excitedly pointing to the Snodgrass Information Processor. "Listen to this. It says that as recently as six months ago, there was an article in a German newspaper about someone remaining underwater for a period of five hours in such a machine."

Griffin paced around the table, his thoughts whizzing around in his head. "And if that's the case, perhaps what we're dealing with is a submersible machine capable of being under water that much time or more. Maybe, to keep it secret, it was designed to look like a monster. Maybe there's a criminal mastermind at work!"

Snodgrass snorted and gave Griffin one of his characteristically skeptical looks. "By 'mastermind,' are you are referring to Professor Moriarity in those Holmes stories? Well, I, for one, remain unconvinced that such a person exists."

Before Griffin could reply, Snodgrass held up his finger for silence. "However, I do think that your notion of a submersible machine has merit. I believe that in order to discover more about this mystery, I shall have to devise something that will allow us to travel underwater ourselves."

His uncle's brow furrowed, and his expression turned

thoughtful. "Yes," he said in distracted mumble. "There have been rumors of hidden tunnels beneath the Thames. I wonder . . ."

Griffin decided that he'd asked his uncle enough questions for one evening. It was probably a good time to withdraw from his uncle's workroom and allow him some time to think.

Griffin's mind was filled with exciting questions, both inspired by his uncle's miraculous inventions and the strange mystery that was starting to unravel. Who was behind the disappearance of Frederick Dent, and why had he been kidnapped? Griffin felt certain that it had something to do with the mysterious client whom Mrs. Dent had mentioned was asking about a clock. But who he was and what he'd really wanted with the clockmaker were still a mystery. After all, it didn't make any sense that someone would want to kidnap a clockmaker when you could hire one in every neighborhood.

As he reached the top of the stairway that led to his room, Griffin's hand moved to his jacket pocket. He'd slipped a scone in his pocket during tea, knowing he'd be hungry later. But since they had the whole basket of goodies from Mrs. Dent waiting downstairs, he figured he might as well enjoy it now. When he pulled out the pastry, he noticed several of the tattered pieces of red paper he'd found earlier sticking to it. As he picked them off, he was suddenly struck by a thought.

His eyes grew wide. Why hadn't he seen it before? If what he thought was true, then everything suddenly made sense. It was all connected!

Seized by the sudden need to prove his theory, Griffin raced downstairs and paused only to tell his uncle that he would be back within the hour. Snodgrass was so deep into designing his latest invention, Griffin didn't think he noticed him leave.

As he chewed his scone and flagged down a hansom cab, Griffin realized an important truth. If what he deduced turned out to be true, then the world as everyone knew it could be changed forever.

THE LIMEHOUSE DOCKS

The Limehouse Docks were a seedy, disreputable part of London that even in bright daylight seemed to be cloaked in shadows. Crimes that happened near the docks seldom saw police action, for even the law enforcement avoided the area as much as they could. It was a place ruled by criminals, and one of the few places in London where they had the upper hand.

Griffin, of course, knew nothing about it. He'd seen the area referenced in the newspaper his uncle had been reading as they'd traveled to the Angler's Club. When he'd realized something about the tattered red paper he'd had in his pocket, he knew the Docks would probably be the best place to get some answers. Unfortunately, as the cab stopped and he climbed out, he began to see that he might have made an error in judgment.

The docks were clearly not the kind of place for a twelve-year-old boy to wander around alone. The dark, twisting lanes and alleys that branched off of the main road were so creepy that it didn't take much imagination to picture what horrible things might be lurking down any one of them. Old men sat on crumbling stoops in front of weathered buildings. They cackled as he passed, commenting in Chinese. Like the area down by the Angler's Club, the entire place reeked of fish, and probably something worse. Griffin tried his best not to breathe as he hurried along, avoiding eye contact with everyone.

Fortunately for Griffin, the kind of place he was looking for was not in short supply. Near the water, next to a moldy wharf, was a shack of an old building with a sign lettered both in Chinese and English that read "LiuYang Imports. Fireworks a specialty." Feeling nervous, but trying to keep focused on what he'd come there to do, Griffin pushed open the shopkeeper's door and entered the dingy, incense-filled shop.

"*Ni Hao*," said a voice.

Griffin recognized it as the Chinese word for greeting. It had come from somewhere in the shadowy area in the back of the shop, and he couldn't make out whether the person who said it was male or female.

Griffin moved closer and saw a very old woman dressed in silk robes, perched behind a counter. Her fingernails were so long they curled back in upon themselves. Her face looked like a dried apple, and fifteen wispy hairs clung to her chin.

Stacked behind her were rows upon rows of fireworks. Griffin noticed twenty-six great rockets covered with golden dragons, thirty-seven Roman candles, and over five hundred twenty-seven tiny explosives no bigger than his pinky. He'd been so nervously counting things that he had to force himself to stop and answer the woman behind the counter.

"Excuse me," Griffin said. "I wonder if you can help me with this." He reached inside his jacket pocket and pulled out the tiny red scraps of paper. "Do you happen to have any fireworks that are covered with paper like this?"

The woman drew a kerosene lantern close and squinted at the paper Griffin held. He couldn't help wondering what would happen if the lamp tipped over. Judging by the amount of fireworks in the shop, he felt certain that the entire city would be blown to kingdom come.

The woman picked up one of the scraps and sniffed it. Suddenly her eyes grew very wide.

"Where did you get these?" she croaked. Griffin noticed that she'd switched from Chinese to perfect English.

"I found them near the river. Can you tell me what kind of fireworks they came from?"

"Very rare," she said slowly. "This paper is used specifically for the Emperor's celebrations. These fireworks contain a secret mixture of black powder crafted by a special group of artisans. Highly explosive."

She handed the scraps back to Griffin, who placed them back in his pocket.

"Do you have any I could buy?" Griffin asked.

"No, no, they are too rare and expensive. We almost never get them in," the old woman answered and then frowned at him, shaking her finger in an admonishing way. "What's a boy like you doing here at this late hour? The Limehouse is no place to be after dark. Bad people roam the streets. You should go home!"

Griffin thanked the woman and promised that he would do just that. After leaving the shop, Griffin strode back the way he'd come, trying his best to stay near the well-lit area by the gas lamps. He was sure he could find a cab eventually.

Griffin's suspicion about the fireworks paper had proven true. But he'd had no idea how powerful the explosives were. If what the woman in the shop said was accurate, then the disappearance of the fireworks that had been written about in the *Times* was definitely related to the special paper he'd found. *After all,* he reasoned, *the Chinese ship was filled with treasures from the Emperor's palace. It makes sense that these rare fireworks came from the same place.*

But thieves hadn't stolen just a few fireworks for a celebration; they had taken the entire cargo. Somebody was planning on blowing something up, and it was bound to be something big. Griffin also had an idea of why the criminals had kidnapped Frederick Dent, but he wanted to check his uncle's Information Processor to be sure. He needed to get back to Baker Street, and fast!

The fog had rolled in, blanketing the crumbling buildings and causing the gas lamps to glow eerily in the twilight. Griffin suddenly realized that he'd somehow strayed from the main road while lost in thought. Nothing around him looked familiar. Worst of all, he couldn't see or hear anyone else on the entire street. He walked faster, trying to make his footfalls as silent as possible.

Suddenly a figure stepped out of a dark alley behind him. Griffin caught a glimpse of the man's shadow in the corner of his eye and sped up. Seconds later he could hear heavy footfalls echoing his own, the stranger's quick stride easily keeping pace with his shorter legs.

Please, oh please, let there be a cab around here, he prayed. But no matter where he looked everything was deserted.

He broke into a run and turned abruptly down a nearby

street, hoping to lose his pursuer. Chinese lanterns overhead gave a reddish, fiery glow to the streets. Griffin was seized with a panic so profound that he almost couldn't breathe. He began counting every random thing he saw as he jogged, trying desperately to calm down. Three alley cats . . . fifteen shards of glass . . . twenty-six gin bottles . . . one rusty knife . . .

A rusty knife! Griffin snatched the knife from the grimy cobblestones. Wheeling around, he faced his pursuer.

But to his surprise, there was no sign of anyone behind him. The fog had cleared enough for him to see a good way down the street, and it was empty. He stared for a few seconds, his breath coming in loud, ragged gasps.

Then a welcome sound suddenly echoed from behind him. It was the unmistakable *clip, clop* of horses' hooves! He jerked his head around and saw a hansom cab winding its way up the street.

"Hello! Wait!" Griffin shouted, dashing after the retreating vehicle. It stopped as the driver looked to see who was yelling.

Griffin raced forward as fast as he could and leapt inside the cab. After slamming the door firmly behind him, he breathed a quick prayer of thanks and sat back in the cushioned chair. Looking down he noticed that his hand still clenched the dagger and seemed unable to let it go.

The cabbie opened the trap and gazed down at him. "What are you playing at, boy, running around the Limehouse Docks at this time of night? It's lucky I heard you, or you might have found yourself dead by morning!"

Griffin gazed up at the portly driver while fumbling in his pocket for what was left of his money. He pulled out all his remaining coins and, handing them to him, said, "Baker Street, please. And hurry!"

The cabbie's eyes grew wide when he saw the fear on Griffin's face. He asked no more questions and hurried the horses forward. Griffin's pounding heart was finally slowing down to normal when he glanced back for one last look behind him. What he saw standing there chilled him to the bone.

There, about fifty meters away, was the shadow of his pursuer. Griffin stared at it, his eyes wide with fear, trying to take in any details he could. But it was too dark and foggy for him to make out anything other than the general size and shape of the man.

As the carriage made its way up the street, the fog rolled back in and hid the mysterious shadow from sight.

Mr. Jackson stared after the departing cab for a second or two. Then he stepped into a nearby alley, hopped on his waiting horse, and took off after the retreating cab. He moved carefully, staying out of sight, but following nonetheless.

But what Jackson didn't know was that there was another shadow who watched them both, a long, thin shadow that, as it stared after them, lit the bowl of a curved, meerschaum pipe.

The flame flickered briefly, and as it did, it illuminated the hawk-like face and high forehead of Sherlock Holmes. Then the great detective pulled his cloak tighter about his shoulders and lowered his deerstalker's hat.

Holmes's intelligent eyes glittered in the darkness as he considered what he'd just seen. Then, with hardly a sound, the great detective disappeared down a side alley, his long legs striding into the darkness, like a bloodhound hot on the trail of some new scent.

THE PLOT THICKENS

Uncle, Uncle!" Griffin gasped as he raced into the parlor at 221A Baker Street. Snodgrass, who was welding his latest invention, doused his torch and raised his welding mask when he noticed Griffin's frightened expression. "What is it? What happened to you?" he said.

"I was at the Limehouse Docks," Griffin said. "I was investigating some clues. But while I was there, somebody tried to follow me. I barely escaped."

"Clues? What clues?" Snodgrass said. He set down his welding mask and torch and gave the boy an irritated glare. "What is this all about? You shouldn't have gone to Limehouse without telling me first! Have you any idea how dangerous it is? What were you thinking?"

"I'm sorry. I didn't know," Griffin said. "But look . . . look what I discovered . . ."

Griffin reached into his pocket and removed the small, red scraps of paper. After handing them to him, he proceeded to tell his uncle where the woman in the fireworks shop said they were from.

Snodgrass clenched his forehead, trying to process the information.

"So what you're saying is that these papers belong to a special type of highly explosive firework, the same kind that was stolen from the Chinese ship. And it's all because someone is planning to make—"

"A bomb!" finished Griffin. "Yes, Uncle. I believe that the reason Frederick Dent was kidnapped was because he's an expert clockmaker. Whoever the culprits are, they intend to make a time bomb so huge that it could devastate London."

Snodgrass stared at Griffin, looking skeptical. "But why Dent? There are hundreds of clockmakers in London. Besides, time bombs are commonplace. It wouldn't take an expert clockmaker to make one."

"That's exactly what I wanted to ask your Information Processor. I suspect that there's something special about Frederick Dent that we don't know about."

Griffin went over to his uncle's machine and turned it on. Snodgrass followed. After the screen began to glow and the familiar text appeared, Griffin typed in the words, *Who is Frederick Dent?*

The machine emitted several puffs of steam while it worked. Griffin bit his pinky nail, waiting for the result. Finally, after what seemed a full minute later, the answer appeared.

Frederick Dent, clockmaker, who, with his father, Edward, was famous for building the Westminster Clock in which the famous bell called Big Ben resides.

Griffin and his uncle stared at the glowing screen, neither of them speaking about what they'd read. Griffin's mind raced. The implications were bigger than he'd ever imagined!

"Impossible," Snodgrass said. "I refuse to believe it."

Griffin looked up at his uncle with a worried expression. "But think about it, Uncle. If Frederick Dent designed the clock, he would be the one who knew it best. What if criminals are forcing him to convert the Westminster Clock Tower into the biggest time bomb ever made?"

Snodgrass's face twitched in annoyance. Griffin suspected that believing in something so grand and far-fetched was difficult for him.

"Speculation, boy. Pure speculation." Snodgrass paced around the room, rubbing his forehead. "The two crimes are completely unrelated. Besides, transporting that many explosives to such a public place would be absolutely impossible," he growled.

"I admit that I haven't figured everything out yet. But if I'm right, then thousands of Londoners could be at terrible risk," Griffin said.

Snodgrass appeared to be pondering his nephew's words.

After a moment, he spoke, "This whole case bears further investigation before we form any conclusions. The first matter of business is to figure out where he was taken. We know he was transported underwater, and, since there have been no other Nessie sightings, he must have been released into some sort of cave or secret dock. I have heard rumors about there being underground tunnels beneath the Thames. Perhaps that's where he's being held."

"But if Dent were just kidnapped, then why hasn't there been a ransom note?" said Griffin. "I would think that whoever did it would have expressed their demands in some kind of letter by now. So they must want something else from him."

Since his uncle seemed to be considering what he was saying, Griffin pressed on, sharing his observations. "Also, James Dunn said he heard gunshots after the monster swallowed Mr. Dent." Griffin pointed to the red scraps of paper in his uncle's hand. "And the red paper I found on the shore means that someone set off fireworks at the bank. Maybe the people who took Mr. Dent wanted to scare off any witnesses."

Snodgrass scowled. "I admit those are things to consider as well."

He directed Griffin over to the device he'd been welding when he walked in. As Griffin drew close, Snodgrass held up a large brass helmet for him to inspect. "Hopefully these helmets will help us gather the extra information we need."

Griffin gazed at the huge brass helmet. It had a single glass window in its front, a small brass box attached to the back of it, and looked extraordinarily heavy.

"What is it?" Griffin asked.

"A diving helmet," Snodgrass replied. Then after a moment he added, "The Snodgrass Submersible . . . er . . . Underwater Utility . . . oh, I'll call it something or other. I haven't figured out an official name for it yet." He indicated the box on the back of the helmet. "I've created a small pump that will provide us with a constant supply of air. When connected to a hose that runs to the surface, we should be able to remain submerged indefinitely."

"Wonderful!" said Griffin, clapping his hands. "Brilliant! Let's go at once!"

As Griffin turned to head back out, he felt his uncle's big hand grab the back of his jacket.

"Oh no you don't," Snodgrass said. "It's no use going before dawn. The Thames is a murky river under the best of circumstances, and swimming in it at night would be completely useless."

Griffin shifted his feet impatiently and scowled up at his uncle. It was hard to wait, considering what might be at stake. Even though it seemed Snodgrass remained skeptical, Griffin felt a nagging certainty that his theories were true.

Snodgrass released his nephew's coat. His expression softened, and he gave Griffin the barest hint of a smile. "Your courage is admirable, Griffin, and your theory, though a little far-fetched, might still prove itself," he said.

Then he sighed and rubbed a hand across his eyes. "But I, for one, have a hard time believing that such a thing is possible. My own theory is that there could be something else at work. Perhaps Dent had problems with creditors or had made powerful foreign enemies."

Griffin didn't think so, but didn't express his opinion further. His uncle turned down the gas lamp and ushered him from the workroom and off to bed.

"We'll leave at first light. I think it would be best if you got to bed and tried to sleep so you'll be prepared for tomorrow. Swimming is difficult work, after all."

He poked Griffin in the shoulder with his forefinger. "And promise me you won't do any more sneaking about, running after clues without informing me first." He gave Griffin an even look. "If your mother ever got word about what you'd done, she'd give me no end of grief!"

"Yes, Uncle."

Griffin bade his uncle good night. But after getting ready for bed, he had a hard time falling asleep. After what seemed like ages, he drifted off to a fitful sleep, but he had nightmare after nightmare. Shadow men chased him through cobblestone streets, and Chinese fireworks, larger than buildings, exploded at his every footfall. Griffin cried out in his sleep, voicing his fears and rehearsing his theories, worrying through the night that he might be too late to stop the terrible tragedy at hand.

And little did he know that as he slept, a shadow, the same one that had followed him all the way from Limehouse and had been crouching under the window of the parlor, listening, was now creeping through the darkened streets.

JACKSON REPORTS

Deep beneath the River Thames there was indeed a network of tunnels. The most famous one was built by a man named Marc Brunel in 1843 and ran from Rotherhithe to Wapping. However, there were other secret passages that ran like rabbit warrens beneath the city. The type of people who used these tunnels were mostly disreputable folk who had secrets to hide or stolen goods to smuggle.

But besides the tunnels, there was something even darker and more secret below the river. Underground compounds flourished and had been occupied by some of the most fearsome criminal lords in England over the course of history. The most famous of these masterminds was Professor James Moriarty. Like that of a great spider, his web of criminal activity was woven throughout all of London and extended to remote parts of Europe and even as far as America.

But the Professor needed help—trusted assistants who could carry out his plans. And none was more trusted than his cousin Nigel. Nigel Moriarity sat, hands folded across his lap, staring at a blazing fire. His headquarters, an opulent underground bunker, was richly decorated.

Deep walnut paneling with gold filigree, rich leather couches, and expensive oil paintings were tastefully positioned around his gigantic office. If his cousin were the Napoleon of Crime, then Nigel was his La Salle. He was the commander of the Underworld, the king of thieves, and as he sat, pondering the great task to which he had been trusted, he smiled.

Staring into the flames, he saw the future of London. It burned as the logs burned; the embers were the screams of thousands that floated upon the night air.

Once the bomb is in place, my cousin's greatest strategic move will be accomplished. And then, finally, we'll checkmate our most troublesome enemy.

Nigel's thoughts were interrupted by a light knock at his door. A man dressed all in black opened the door and slipped into the room. It was the same shadow that had been following Griffin Sharpe a few hours earlier.

"Sorry to disturb you, sir," the hulking man said.

"Not at all, Jackson. What have you discovered?" Nigel asked.

The man removed his large-brimmed hat and held it nervously in his hands. His face was a mess of scars, pitted and lined from countless fights.

"The boy, sir. The one from America."

"Go on."

"He's a clever one, he is. He and that Snodgrass bloke are onto us. They plan on diving into the Thames tomorrow to see if they can locate Dent."

Nigel Moriarity didn't say anything for a long moment. So

long, in fact, that Jackson began to get nervous and wondered if he should leave. Like a dog that knew its master well, Jackson was smart enough to know that bad news was often accompanied by terrible outbursts.

But this time there were no tantrums. Instead, Nigel turned and gave Jackson a cold smile.

"Then we shall be ready to greet them when they arrive. Notify the frogmen."

PREPARATIONS

G riffin and his uncle were up well before dawn. Neither one had been able to sleep soundly. They were too nervous and excited. But they wouldn't be able to see anything in the river until daylight, so they were stuck with a couple of hours of anxious waiting.

Thankfully, Snodgrass had sent Watts out for groceries the night before, and he and Griffin were able to enjoy a decent cup of early morning tea.

God bless Mrs. Dent, Griffin thought as he sipped the hot liquid and munched on the last of the leftover scones from Mrs. Dent's basket. His eyes were puffy from lack of sleep, and he felt nervous and jumpy. The tea helped calm him a little, and he was grateful for it. If it weren't for the money Mrs. Dent had provided when they'd taken the case, he'd probably be sipping the horrible, watery stuff that his uncle had been drinking for weeks. And he didn't even want to think about what he might be eating.

Snodgrass looked up from the newspaper he was reading. He was dressed in his usual attire, an old tweed jacket and trousers. Griffin noticed that today he wore an unusual tiepin that looked like it had tiny metal gears welded to it.

Snodgrass noticed Griffin's glance and, pointing to it, mentioned, "It was given to me by the Edinburgh Engineering Guild. I used to be a charter member before I, er, embarked on other pursuits."

Griffin realized that there was much about his uncle he didn't know. He wondered about his uncle's past—like why he'd decided to become an investigator and how he'd learned to make such incredible inventions. But he wasn't sure that it was proper to ask such personal questions. *I wonder what happened between him and my mother? And why did he say that they weren't close?*

His musings were interrupted by the sound of Watts clanking into the kitchen with a pot of freshly boiled tea. Griffin held out his cup and watched as the butler expertly poured him a steaming cup. He still couldn't get over how amazing the machine was.

"Thank you," Griffin said. Watts's blue eyes glowed in response, and he nodded politely.

"Oh, Watts, please bring us the pastries you bought at Tottingham's yesterday," Snodgrass said. "There's a good fellow."

The robot dutifully set down the teapot he was carrying and disappeared into the pantry. At the sound of the word *pastry*, Griffin glanced up from his teacup, giving his uncle a surprised look.

He felt sure his uncle saw his expression, but Snodgrass pretended not to notice and continued to sip his tea and scan the headlines of the morning paper. Watts returned shortly, carrying a tray filled with some of the delicious-looking pastries Griffin had seen in Tottingham's shop when he'd first arrived.

The mechanical butler set the pastries down on the table, and Griffin couldn't help smiling. Piled high on the tray were little pies filled with raspberry jam, buttered scones with plump raisins, and flaky, moon-shaped pastries his uncle informed him were called *croissants*.

Griffin couldn't decide which to try first. His uncle reached from behind the paper, took one of the scones, and with his face hidden behind the paper said casually, "If you'd rather have blood sausage, I'm sure Watts could manage it."

Griffin chuckled. *No chance of that!*

He was beginning to understand his uncle. Like a cactus, Rupert Snodgrass was prickly on the outside, but hidden beneath the spines was a soft interior. Griffin knew that his uncle had specifically ordered this breakfast as a way of showing him that he cared.

And the gesture was not lost on Griffin.

"Thank you, Uncle," Griffin said. Snodgrass replied with a friendly grunt from behind his newspaper.

They both ate in silence for a few minutes. In spite of the wonderful breakfast, Griffin was beginning to feel more and more anxious about continuing the investigation. Who knew how many lives were at stake, or when the villains would strike? It was terrible having to wait, but it also felt terrible to face unknown danger. Griffin just wanted to get started so that he wouldn't have to keep thinking about it.

He glanced outside and saw that it wouldn't be too much longer before dawn. There was no clock in the kitchen, but he guessed by the color of the sky that it was probably around five o'clock in the morning. He thought about the shadowy figure that had chased him at the Limehouse Docks and wondered what other dangers might be in store. It was obvious to him that whoever the criminals were, they had to be capable of extreme violence.

"Uncle?"

"Yes?"

Griffin nibbled on his pastry a bit before continuing. Then he asked in a worried voice, "What if we should have to defend ourselves? I . . . I'm afraid that I'm not very good at fighting."

Snodgrass took a long sip of tea. Then, after lowering his paper, said, "Not to worry, lad, I've already taken precautions."

Griffin fidgeted in his chair. All of the fights he'd ever been in had ended with him on the ground, nursing a black eye.

Snodgrass continued, "Being a detective is not for the faint-hearted. When you stir up a hornet's nest, you're bound to get a few stings. However, I have something in mind for you that might help you feel more confident should we have to fight."

He led Griffin back to the workroom. Griffin noticed that positioned next to the two finished diving helmets was a plain-looking, wooden box. Snodgrass handed it to his nephew. Griffin opened the lid and saw that resting on a silken pillow was one of the futuristic-looking weapons he'd seen hanging on his uncle's wall. The small, ornate pistol had a glass vial protruding from the top of its barrel. And inside the vial bubbled a glowing, green, viscous fluid.

"The Snodgrass Stinger is not a toy," Griffin's uncle said. Snodgrass pointed at the glass tube. "Inside that vial is a nonlethal chemical that will render an attacker inert for a period of twenty-four hours. Simply point the weapon at your adversary and pull the trigger; you don't have to do anything else."

Griffin lifted the weapon carefully from the box. It felt heavy in his palm, but fit his hand nicely. Looking at it more closely, he noticed the carefully crafted walnut handle and the etched filigree that decorated the gun's barrel. He was glad that it wasn't supposed to kill anybody.

"Thank you, Uncle," Griffin said. "And please don't think me ungrateful, but I certainly hope I won't have to use it."

Snodgrass nodded approvingly and said, "And that's the proper way to approach the use of any weapon. It should only be used as a last resort."

He spent another ten minutes carefully instructing Griffin in the proper way to fire and carry the unusual weapon, and, by the time they were done, Griffin felt reasonably confident that he could defend himself if he had to.

As the sun finally rose, throwing long shadows down the London streets, Griffin found himself wearing a waterproof diving suit over his clothes and heading back to the River Thames. He suddenly wished that he hadn't eaten so many pastries at breakfast. His stomach flip-flopped awkwardly as they walked outside the Angler's Club, and Griffin caught the now familiar aroma of spoiled mackerel.

Whatever happens, Griffin thought, *after this case is done, I never want to see or smell another fish as long as I live.*

19

WHAT LIES BENEATH

The plunge into the icy water of the Thames nearly took Griffin's breath away. The waterproof suit that Snodgrass had fashioned the night before wasn't as effective as he'd promised. Within moments of diving into the river, ice water seeped through the fabric, and Griffin was soaked and freezing.

He gasped, and was thankful that when he did, he was able to draw breath. Fortunately for Griffin, his underwater helmet worked perfectly, pumping fresh air in and allowing him to breathe underwater. Doing his best to ignore the cold water, Griffin gazed through the murky depths around him. He marveled at being able to breathe as naturally as if he were on land. His father had taught him to swim at a young age, but the Atlantic Ocean was even colder than the Thames, so Griffin hadn't spent a great deal of time practicing his strokes.

Through the murky water, Griffin could see his uncle swimming toward him. As he drew closer, Snodgrass waved his hand and, pointing downward, motioned for them to go deeper. As they swam toward the bottom of the river, Griffin noticed that his uncle carried a long spear with an unusual tip on it, something that Snodgrass said was electrically charged and would provide them with additional protection. It had a specially designed, insulated handle that protected the bearer while underwater.

Unconsciously, Griffin's hand strayed to his side, ensuring that he had the Stinger securely strapped to his waist. He hoped that the waterproof holster he wore would keep the weapon from getting too waterlogged to work.

They swam downward, looking for clues. As they descended, Griffin could feel the water pressure mounting all around him, but it didn't bother him too much. What did disarm him was the eerie silence, broken only by the tiny hiss of the steam-driven pump that forced fresh air into his helmet.

When they drew near to the bottom of the river, the murkiness vanished and Griffin was able to see clearly through the helmet's window. However, being at such depths and relying on a hastily constructed piece of machinery to keep him safe made Griffin feel very nervous. He couldn't help counting everything he saw. *Three boulders, one old piece of pottery, two fishing lures, thirteen mussels . . .*

He tried not to think about the long, delicate hose that was connected to his helmet, providing his only source of air from the surface. He forced himself not to worry about what would happen if the pump failed or a bird landed on the other end of his breathing tube.

He focused on numbers and tried to calm himself down. *One old cannon, three rusty rivets . . . five men in diving suits . . .*

WHAT?

He looked again. Sure enough, in the distance, he saw five

figures approaching, swimming toward them and wearing suits of a similar design as his. Griffin stared, unable to believe what he was seeing, but quickly realized that these men were not out diving for recreation; they were obviously coming for them! His perceptive gaze instantly measured the size and strength of each enemy; the strange-looking, crossbow-styled weapons they carried; and who was leading the charge.

Griffin and his uncle were woefully outmatched. He fumbled at his waist for his pistol, ready to try using it in spite of being underwater. But because it had been strapped in tightly and his hands were so cold from the freezing water, Griffin couldn't unfasten the buttons that held it shut with his numb fingers.

As the enemy divers approached, Snodgrass swung out with the long spear. The nearest diver was caught off guard as a bright flash shot from its tip, sending a cascade of electricity into his body. Seeing his comrade so easily dispatched, the leader, a ferocious brute, motioned for his other divers to surround Snodgrass and stay clear of his weapon.

Griffin didn't know what to do. He wanted to help his uncle, but without the aid of his weapon, he felt completely helpless. He looked around, trying to find anything he could use to defend himself. Then he spotted a large rock on the river bottom. He dove down and scooped it up in his arms. The rock was big and slowed him down as he swam, but he was too panicked to notice. All he could think of was trying to rescue his uncle before the divers shot him with their underwater crossbows.

As he rushed forward, he couldn't help counting the bolts on the divers' helmets, the barbs on their arrows, and the unusual patterns painted on the sides of their black suits. He raised the rock, intending to smash the large brass tank that clung to the nearest diver's back. But just as he was about to bring the rock down, the diver turned, pointing his deadly arrow at Griffin's chest.

Griffin had no choice but to drop the stone. Out of the corner of his eye, he saw it plunge down to the river bottom, and it seemed that as it went down, his hope went with it. He raised his hands above his head in surrender with only one thing on his mind, a single phrase that kept repeating itself over and over again. *If I'm about to die, then, Lord, please let it be quick!*

THE SECRET LAIR

They were escorted to a crumbling canal entrance deep under the water. As they entered the tunnel, Griffin felt the air in his breathing tube shut off. Because the line could no longer reach the surface, there was no way for him to get any oxygen!

He tried not to panic, knowing that if he did, he would lose even more air. Instead, he focused on the growing light in front of them and swam toward it with long, purposeful strokes. They emerged in a large pool in an underground cavern. Snodgrass hastily undid the clamps that secured Griffin's helmet to his suit and then quickly undid his own. The two gasped for breath, taking in deep gulps of fresh air as quickly as they were able.

They'd hardly recovered before they felt rough hands shove them in the back. They were pushed out of the shallows onto a rough-hewn path. Griffin saw that the divers had Snodgrass's weapon and, looking down, saw that they'd removed his pistol while he'd been trying to catch his breath.

"Now move!" the leader said, his voice muffled inside his helmet.

Griffin and his uncle were marched down the pathway, with weapons pointed at their backs. As they walked deeper into the cave, Griffin stole glances at the rocky walls, wondering how long the secret cave had existed. It seemed like they were miles below the earth, but he knew that it couldn't be so.

After several minutes of trudging along, Griffin saw an area to his left open up into an immense cavern. He gasped when he saw what was inside.

Floating in the middle of a giant, underground lake was the monster that had started the whole mystery. The thing was surrounded on all sides by gigantic urns filled with some kind of flaming substance that cast eerie, green light around the cavern and made it look even more frightening. He could easily see how it had inspired such terror in the fisherman, James Dunn. It was a mechanical marvel, a gigantic submarine that if taken at a glance would certainly have resembled drawings of the famous Loch Ness Monster.

Rising high above the submarine's rounded back was a long crane fitted with huge iron jaws. They were easily as large as a man, and Griffin felt sure that they had snatched Frederick Dent from where he stood on the beach and had made James Dunn think he was witnessing a monster eating its prey.

Workers surrounded it on all sides and were polishing its black, anodized metal sides. Others were positioned on its decks, welding new fittings in place. The bright sparks from the torches produced a frightening effect, causing a giant shadow on the cavern wall to look very much like a sea monster.

Well, that's one deduction I got right, at least, Griffin thought. He glanced over at his uncle, and Snodgrass nodded at Griffin, acknowledging his discovery, and Griffin, in spite of the scary circumstances that they were in, managed a tiny smile.

They turned down another corridor, and this one opened into a long hallway. Lining every side of the tunnel were huge crates, and Griffin, spotting the Chinese characters painted on the sides, knew them to be the explosives stolen from the Limehouse Docks.

That's two! he counted to himself. Now all that remained to be proven was his theory about Frederick making the Westminster tower into the world's largest time bomb. Although he took private pleasure at being right, he hoped he would be wrong about his third guess. It was too horrible to think about.

They walked down some crudely cut steps and found themselves inside a dank, brick-lined room. Griffin felt a chill when he saw several cells with heavy, rusting bars lining the walls. Griffin and his uncle were forced inside a foul-smelling cell at the end of the corridor. As the bars clanked shut behind him, he felt a terrible panic well up inside of him. The prospect of being helpless to stop the terrible tragedy at hand was almost too much to bear. The thought of never seeing his family again or experiencing the sunshine on his face suddenly made him panic.

Griffin raced to the bars and shook them with all his might. "No!" he shouted. "Please, let me out! Let me out!"

But nobody listened to his anguished plea.

MR. FREDERICK DENT

T his couldn't have gone any better," said Rupert Snodgrass.

Griffin whirled from where he stood, gripping the bars of his cell.

"How so, Uncle?" he said, his voice rising in panic. "We're in prison with no way out, and those . . . those foul men are going to blow up half of London!"

"But we have found what we were looking for," said Snodgrass with a triumphant smile. "And, most importantly, we've solved the case before my *neighbor* ever found out about it!"

Griffin thought that his uncle looked happier than he'd ever seen him. There was a gleam in his eye as he rocked back and forth like a child unable to contain his excitement. Snodgrass then gestured to the back of the cell, where, for the first time, Griffin saw a man standing.

The man was round in the middle and had bushy sideburns on either side of his long face. Waves of snowy hair cascaded from his brow, and his eyes glittered with intelligence. His suit, which Griffin could tell was expensive, looked a bit worn, which he assumed was probably from sleeping on the stone floor of the cell. But the man appeared otherwise to be in good health.

"Allow me to introduce Mr. Frederick Dent," Snodgrass said proudly. "Mr. Dent, this is Master Sharpe."

Griffin stared at the man in shock. Here he was, the person they'd been sent to find, standing right in front of them! Recovering his composure and feeling slightly embarrassed about his panicked outburst, Griffin stepped forward and shook the man's outstretched hand.

"I'm very pleased to make your acquaintance, sir," he said politely.

"My word, you're an American!" Mr. Dent said. Then turning to Snodgrass he asked, "What the deuce are you two gentlemen doing here? I didn't think they would need anyone else for their plan."

Snodgrass shook his head gravely. "Actually, we were hired by your wife to find you. My name is Snodgrass, Rupert Snodgrass, and I am a private investigator."

The man studied Snodgrass for a moment and then threw up his hands in mock despair. "Well, now you've found me, haven't you? And it looks like we're all prisoners."

Griffin spied something in the corner of the cell that caught his attention. Curled up on the floor was a long piece of paper. Griffin knew at once what it was, but hesitated to ask. After a few minutes he couldn't stand the suspense any longer, and, dreading what he might hear as the answer, he turned to Mr. Dent and asked, "Pardon me, sir, but are those blueprints?"

Frederick Dent looked at where Griffin was pointing.

"Why, yes, they are. As a matter of fact, drawing those was the reason I was brought to this horrible place."

Griffin's heart sank. He knew without looking what was printed on them.

Mr. Dent retrieved the plans from the corner of the cell and displayed them for Griffin and his uncle to see. There, drawn in great detail, was the Westminster Clock Tower.

"They've forced me to do it, you see," he explained. "They told me that Sarah would be killed if I didn't comply with their wishes. Every day they take me from the cell to work on the plans. I've nearly finished."

"And what exactly is it that they requested you do?" Snodgrass asked.

Frederick Dent suddenly looked nervous. He gazed down at the floor and his hands shook.

"To help them destroy Sherlock Holmes, the Queen, and half of London."

SNOOPS

Griffin watched his uncle's triumphant expression crumble when Dent said "Sherlock Holmes," and he sagged against the wall of the cell.

"When is this supposed to happen?" Griffin asked Mr. Dent.

"At twelve o'clock precisely," the man said nervously, "the Queen is conducting a ceremony to honor Sherlock Holmes at Westminster Palace. When the clock strikes the hour, the bomb will detonate."

"But, sir. Think of the consequences!" Griffin said. "All the lives that will be lost! Without the Queen, the country will be thrown into chaos."

"I . . . I had no choice," said Dent, looking anguished. "If I didn't help them, they'd kill Sarah!"

Their conversation was interrupted by the sound of footsteps echoing on the flagstone floor.

"They're coming!" said Dent. He motioned for Griffin to stay quiet.

Griffin stared out between the bars. Soon two burly-looking

guards approached the cell. They were dressed completely in black, and as Griffin studied the larger of the two, a chill went up his spine. His height and stance were exactly as Griffin remembered. It was the same shadowy figure that had chased him at the docks!

"You, out!" the man barked, pointing at Dent. The portly man nervously tucked the plans under his arm and exited the cell. On his way out, Dent turned toward Griffin and said quietly, "I'm sorry."

Griffin watched as the two guards escorted him down the hall with a sick feeling in the pit of his stomach. He had no idea what time it was, but he estimated that at least a few hours had passed since they had left the apartment at Baker Street. How much time did they have left? The thugs certainly weren't going to release them after the bombing, knowing Griffin and Snodgrass would go straight to Scotland Yard.

Griffin turned back to his uncle. Snodgrass was sitting on the floor of the cell, staring off into space. "What are we going to do?" Griffin asked.

But Snodgrass didn't answer. Griffin walked over to him and shook his shoulder. "Uncle, we have to escape and warn Mr. Holmes!"

"We're not going anywhere," said Snodgrass in a flat voice. "If Holmes is too stupid to know what's going to happen, then let him suffer the consequences."

Griffin stared at him, unable to believe what he was hearing. "You can't possibly mean that!"

Snodgrass didn't respond immediately. But when he finally spoke, his voice was tinged with bitterness. "My parents moved into the apartment at 221 Baker Street when I was a child. At that time, your mother was ten and I was seven. I had a dog . . . a basset hound named Snoops," said Snodgrass. "I had raised him since he was a puppy, and we were constantly together. He had a white, star-shaped pattern on his forehead, and I believed the star meant that he'd been sent from heaven especially for me. He was my closest friend and had been ever since my father died."

Snodgrass sighed. "My mother remarried, to a man who had a daughter . . . your mother. She soon discovered that Snoops was so close to me that we even answered to the same name." Snodgrass chuckled sadly. "I never liked being called Rupert, and my new sister took to calling me Snoops too."

Griffin noticed that his uncle's voice had softened at the memory. His eyes were closed, like he was trying to visualize the past.

"My sister and I attended a terrible school filled with bullies and cruel headmasters. Once I had to rescue her from a gang of ruffians that had torn her dress. The boys were much bigger than I, but I had Snoops with me, and the dog helped me defend her. But neither he, nor I, were much good at fighting . . ."

Snodgrass's voice grew quiet. "They beat me terribly. Nigel, a boy infamous at school for his cruelty to the younger children, grabbed Snoops. I watched helplessly as he grasped him by his long ears and dangled him above the ground. The poor dog's wails were terrible to hear. I—I was helpless to stop them."

Snodgrass voice was gruff with emotion.

"The boys took Snoops away. They had broken my arm and blackened both of my eyes, but all I could think of was my poor dog. My sister tried to comfort me, but I didn't want her to touch me. It was unfair, but I suppose I blamed her for what had happened. I felt that I'd lost my closest friend."

Snodgrass brought a hand to his forehead, a pained expression on his face.

"I heard Snoops's tortured cries over and over in my nightmares that night and for many nights after. And from that day forward, I was determined that I would become a detective, to find my dog and bring the boys to justice. It might sound silly to anyone else, but I never really got over what happened. And even though it's been many years since that day, I've never forgotten it, nor how terrible it felt to be so helpless."

Griffin felt sick. He could imagine how horrible it must have been for his uncle to lose his dog. He knew that sometimes animals understood you in a way people couldn't.

Snodgrass took a deep breath and continued his story. "Two weeks later, Sherlock Holmes moved into the apartment next door. Everyone had heard of the famous detective, even before John Watson started to write his adventures for the *Strand Magazine*. When I heard that he was going to start his agency next door to our apartment, you can imagine how excited I was. Here was someone who would understand and could help me find poor Snoops. It took me nearly a week to gather the courage to knock on his door. I told him my story, and I thought he was going to find my dog."

Griffin saw his uncle's eyes tighten, and his voice grew bitter once more.

"But later I realized that all my hopes had been in vain. When I went back to see if he had found out anything about Snoops, he told me that he couldn't help me after all. He was too busy to help a little boy find his dog. He had other, more important clients to deal with . . . national politics . . . murder. Sherlock Holmes sent me away, not realizing that as he did so he'd created an enemy for life. I could never forgive him for not taking the time to help me."

He turned to Griffin and said, "I determined that ever after, I would beat him at his own game. I would become the better detective. Because there might be other people who've lost things that mattered to them . . . even if they weren't matters of national security. And this time the victims wouldn't be left feeling helpless, without anywhere to turn."

They were silent for a long moment. Griffin finally understood his uncle and why he acted the way he did. He felt a tremendous surge of compassion for him. Their personal stories were more similar than he'd imagined. Griffin knew what it was like to be alone and to hope for someone to understand him. His uncle had lived that way, nursing his hurt and disappointment for years and years.

But Griffin could tell that bitterness had done tremendous damage to his uncle's relationships with people. There was only one solution Griffin could think of that would set him free, and it was something that might be hard for his uncle to accept.

His Uncle Snodgrass had to learn how to forgive.

Praying that God would give him wisdom, Griffin asked tenderly, "Did you ever find Snoops?"

"I never did," his uncle replied.

Griffin thought a moment and then said, "Did you know that when my mother talks of you, she still calls you Snoops?"

Snodgrass remained silent, so he continued, saying, "Growing up, I never really understood why I had an uncle with such an usual name. But I noticed that whenever she mentioned you, she did something peculiar. She would turn her face away. Even when I was little, I thought it was an odd gesture."

Griffin took a deep breath and said gently, "But about a week before I left for my trip to London, I caught a glimpse of her reflection in a window. It was then that I discovered the reason she'd turned away from me all those times. It was to hide the tears in her eyes when she talked about you. She didn't want me to see her cry."

Griffin hesitated and then said slowly, "I could tell that she loved you very much. And after hearing your story, I think she's suffered along with you all of these years. Because when you lost Snoops"—Griffin placed his hand on his uncle's shoulder— "she lost her brother."

Neither of them spoke for a long while. But after sitting in silence for a few minutes, Snodgrass stood and then did something that Griffin never expected. Gazing down at his nephew with his eyes filled with tears, Rupert pulled him into an awkward embrace. Then, after the quick hug, he smiled.

And for the first time since Griffin had met him, it looked as if he were genuinely happy to have him there.

ESCAPE!

T
he lock on the cell door proved to be difficult to pick. Griffin's ever-resourceful uncle had removed some of the reinforced wires in the diving suits and fashioned lock picks out of them. But Snodgrass struggled to open the rusty lock. For a long while nothing happened.

"Come on," Snodgrass muttered as he tried to get the chambers inside the lock to loosen. Griffin wondered how many times his uncle had had to use lock picks in the past. He didn't seem to be an expert at it. After a few more minutes of struggling with the lock, Griffin asked, "Would you like me to try?"

"No, I've got it," Snodgrass replied. He continued to twist and turn the delicate pieces of metal, navigating them inside the hidden chambers.

Griffin sighed and stared out from between the bars. He wanted so badly to get out of the cage that he could hardly stand it.

Then there was a sudden click and the door swung open. Griffin felt a surge of relief. Snodgrass grinned and replaced the wires in his pocket.

"It took a bit, but I got it in the end," he said. Then he raised a warning finger and added, "There's sure to be danger ahead, so stay close."

Griffin didn't have to be told twice. The last thing he wanted right now was to be lost alone in the maze of tunnels!

They quickly made their way down the hall, following the direction that the guards had taken Frederick Dent. After checking to make sure that everything was clear, they entered a nearby guard's station. Inside, they saw that their weapons were lying on a small table.

"Now, that's a surprise," Snodgrass said, handing the pistol to Griffin. "I would have thought the guards would have taken them to use. Maybe they weren't sure how they worked."

Griffin felt relieved to have the Stinger back in his possession. If anybody was going to try to put him back in that cell, he didn't want to go down without a fight.

He checked the pistol for any signs of damage. "Mine looks okay, Uncle. How's yours?" Griffin whispered.

His uncle tested his spear by pulling a small switch at its handle that caused the tip to emit a loud spark. Griffin winced at the electrical crackle, hoping that it wouldn't attract unwanted attention. But his uncle seemed oblivious to the loud noise.

"Jolly good," his uncle said. "It still works." Then he turned to Griffin and motioned him toward the door on the other side of the room.

They exited the guardroom and found themselves in a winding corridor. Unlike the cavelike tunnels they'd taken when they first arrived, this one was paved and its walls were overlaid with bricks. They traveled down the tunnel for several minutes, neither of them knowing for certain if they were headed in the right direction.

The farther down they went, the more anxious and claustrophobic Griffin felt. He tried not to think about the hundreds of feet of earth and water separating him from the surface. Even though it had only been a few hours, it felt like it had been a lifetime since he'd breathed fresh air.

Don't think about it, he warned himself. *You'll just make it worse.*

So he focused instead on counting the numerous bricks that lined the walls as a way to try to calm down. He'd just counted three thousand three hundred sixteen when suddenly they heard the sounds of voices. Listening closely, he realized that they were coming not from behind them, but from a point farther along the passage. Griffin and his uncle shared panicked looks. There was nowhere to hide!

Flattening themselves up against the walls, they waited for whoever it was to round the corner. Griffin crouched near the floor, with the brass pistol clutched firmly in his hand.

Two burly guards strode into view. As soon as they came around the corner, Snodgrass lunged with his spear while Griffin, taking careful aim, fired his pistol.

ZZAAAP! Lightning arced from the tip of Snodgrass's spear. His target flew back, slamming into the brick wall with a sickening *THUD!*

SPLORT! Griffin's stinger belched a glowing bolt of green plasma that splattered onto the second guard, hitting him squarely in the chest.

That's all??? Griffin felt disappointed and a little panicked. The green goop that shot from his gun seemed as ineffective on the hulking brute as being hit by a ball of mud. Surely his uncle hadn't given him something this stupid to defend himself with!

The man Griffin shot looked down with a surprised expression at where the glowing blob had hit him. Then, seeing that there was no bullet wound, he flashed an evil grin at Griffin and advanced.

"I'm going to make you pay for this, boy," the guard cracked.

But he only got three paces before he suddenly lurched forward and slammed to the floor, senseless.

Griffin stared, amazed at what he'd done. Snodgrass walked over to the body and nudged it with the toe of his shoe. Then he glanced up at his nephew and smiled. "Nice shot, lad."

Griffin stared first at his weapon, then down at the unconscious man, who was snoring loudly. "You're sure he'll be all right?" he asked, worried.

"Of course," said Snodgrass. "When he wakes, it will be as if he's had a long night's sleep. Of course, it will have been about twenty-four hours by then, and he might have some nasty bruises, but otherwise he'll never know the difference."

Griffin took another look at the brass pistol. It was a lot more powerful than he'd initially thought! And he was certainly glad that it hadn't hurt the man. He wasn't sure he could handle a weapon that could actually kill someone.

"Come along, Griffin," his uncle hissed. "And look sharp."

"I always do," Griffin quipped. And his uncle flashed him a grin. The boy replaced the pistol in his holster and hurried forward, trying to move as noiselessly as he could.

He hoped that they would find a way out soon. *Time is ticking*, he thought as he raced down the ever-descending tunnel.

Suddenly a piercing whistle split the air. Griffin and Snodgrass both winced and covered their ears.

What's that? Griffin wondered.

BOOOOM! The stone floor beneath their feet rumbled as if they were in the middle of an earthquake. Several bricks from the tunnel ceiling came crashing down, and Griffin covered his head with his arms, hoping that he wouldn't get hit. Through the rubble he glimpsed his uncle, who looked surprised but otherwise unharmed.

Griffin coughed from the avalanche of dust and debris. "What was that?" he said.

Snodgrass, who was in the middle of a coughing fit, didn't reply but motioned for him to follow. Visions of fireworks accidentally exploding or an experimental mishap with some huge piece of machinery filled his head as he jogged along behind his uncle.

I hope the tunnel isn't caving in!

Then, as they turned down a side passage, they found that the tunnel gave way to a huge, well-lit room. Griffin breathed a sigh of relief to be out of the crumbling, narrow tunnel.

Standing at a big table covered with blueprints was Frederick Dent. The big man's head was lowered in dismay. Behind him Griffin saw train tracks heading down a long, dark tunnel. Dust was everywhere.

A train station? Griffin wondered.

Griffin walked forward, and as he did his foot accidentally kicked a small piece of debris, scattering rocks across the floor. At the sound, Dent looked up. Griffin was surprised to see that he'd been crying.

"Mr. Dent! Whatever is the matter?" Griffin asked, rushing

forward. Dent shook his head and gripped the sides of his head in dismay.

"They've gone! And it's all my fault!"

"Where? Where have they gone?" Snodgrass said. "And what made that infernal noise?"

Dent seemed unable to speak, but raised a shaking finger and pointed at the tracks. Griffin noticed an unusual-looking train car positioned there. It was jet-black and looked like no other steam engine he'd ever seen. He realized that the piercing sound he'd heard had been similar to a train whistle. But he still couldn't understand what had made the booming noise that had shaken the entire cavern.

Snodgrass seemed immediately fascinated by the engine and rushed over to examine it more closely.

"This is solid workmanship," he murmured. "Top-notch engineering." He gave Frederick Dent a serious look. "Who is behind all this, Dent?"

Dent gathered his composure and answered, "Someone called Moriarty. He just left with about a dozen of his men. They have the clock tower plans and are putting the final batch of explosives in place as we speak."

Griffin boggled. *Moriarty!* Could it be the real Professor Moriarty from the Sherlock Holmes stories? If that were true, then Griffin knew they were up against the most formidable criminal mind in the world!

He gulped.

If his uncle were similarly impressed, he didn't show it. "Then we must go after them," Snodgrass said simply. He turned back to the engine and asked, "Does this machine work?"

"I believe so," said Dent. "But they seemed reluctant to use it and preferred the other one. I heard Mr. Moriarity mention that he'd designed them both, but he also said something about that one being unpredictable."

"I never knew that he was an inventor," said Rupert Snodgrass.

"I thought you said you didn't believe that there was a Professor Moriarty," Griffin said, but then immediately wished he hadn't. Snodgrass gave him a look of disgust that was similar to the one he'd given him when he'd mentioned the name Sherlock Holmes for the first time.

"I didn't say *exactly* that," Snodgrass replied icily. "It's just that I personally haven't bumped up against him before. I suppose that there's a first time for everything."

Griffin had been around his uncle long enough to know that it would be better to leave the subject of Holmes and anything related to him alone for now. He walked over and looked more closely at the engine, his eyes traveling over its strange, gigantic wheels and brightly polished smokestack. They were different than the ones on a typical steam locomotive. This was a strange configuration that wrapped back around the sides of the engine in long, sweeping curves. The only parts of it that weren't black were the bloodred decorative paint lines that swept across its streamlined body, accentuating its curves.

There was something about it that reminded him of the incredible seagull camera he'd seen back at the River Thames. The engine possessed the same sense of artistry and detail. And looking closer, Griffin noticed that there was a small plate with the initials N. M. engraved on it positioned next to the control panel.

"It does look impressive," said Griffin.

"Yes," said his uncle. "It certainly does."

There was no other way to describe the train engine but to say that it looked fast. Griffin watched as Snodgrass climbed aboard and into the driver's seat.

"We've no time to waste," he said abruptly. "Are you coming?"

Dent looked worried. "Are you comfortable piloting that thing? Moriarty said it was unreliable. Maybe it's going to fly apart as soon as we set off."

Griffin shared a look with his uncle. Then, turning back to Mr. Dent, he said, "I'm afraid that's a chance we're going to have to take, sir." Then, with a grim smile he added, "When you shake up a hornet's nest, you're bound to get a few stings."

MORIARTY

As the engine's wheels screamed to a stop, sending sparks flying behind them, Nigel Moriarty checked his pocket watch. It was 10:15 a.m.

"Excellent," he murmured as he stepped from the luxurious cabin of the powerful black engine and surveyed his elegant invention. Billows of steam rose from the streamlined smokestack, and the wheels practically glowed with friction.

This Rocket Engine was perfect, unlike his previous design. It had traveled from the underground compound, switching tracks at Charring Cross precisely at the time he'd scheduled it to, missing all the other major trains before switching back to a set of secret tracks that led underneath Westminster Palace in just ten point two minutes. And that was even with two cars filled with explosives trailing behind it! It had been tricky, especially designing the secret tracks so that they would be sufficiently camouflaged. The whole plan would have crumbled if anyone had noticed the extra tracks and removed them.

"Shall we begin unloading the cars, Guv?" asked one of his hired goons.

"Yes," Nigel replied. "And be careful!"

The man slouched off to the rest of the waiting thugs and ordered them to begin moving the piles of fireworks from the waiting train car.

Huge crates filled with gigantic rockets were carefully placed on handcarts. Just one of the rockets could blow a hole the size of a hansom cab in the side of the clock, so Nigel watched the unloading carefully. It wouldn't do at all to have an accident now. There were over two tons of fireworks strategically placed inside the clock's mechanisms already, so it was a miracle that there hadn't been any mishaps thus far.

"Go slowly, you dolt!" Nigel hissed at one of his workers who was wheeling a cart recklessly forward. This was no time to get sloppy.

He placed his silk top hat on his head and adjusted his tie. It truly was a momentous occasion. For so many years, his cousin had been trying to defeat Sherlock Holmes. And now, with clever planning and his use of the very latest scientific advancements, Nigel was about to do something the great Professor couldn't do.

Nigel thought about the chaos and destruction that would follow this afternoon's surprise and grinned. He reminded himself that it would be more than just Sherlock Holmes's life that would be forfeit. He'd also be stripping England of her beloved monarch and probably killing countless others.

He sighed in anticipation. By this time tomorrow, he'd be in his secret villa near the Reichenbach Falls, enjoying an expensive feast with all of his favorite dishes and setting his sights on his next goal: the elimination of his cousin and seizing control of his criminal empire.

Professor Moriarty might have been brilliant once, but Nigel knew that he'd never been the same after his encounter with Sherlock Holmes in Switzerland. The two had plunged off the falls, but neither had died. Holmes had survived by his own wits, but the Professor had only survived because of Nigel's ingenuity.

It was he who had invented the machine that had given his cousin life once more. But since the accident, James Moriarty had grown paranoid and had made, in Nigel's estimation, several seriously flawed decisions.

Perhaps it's his wounded pride, Nigel mused. After all, being confined to a steam-driven wheelchair was bound to make someone feel helpless. Maybe the reason his cousin's brilliance had faded was the fact that Holmes had emerged from their battle intact, while he had not.

As a boy, Nigel always looked up to his cousin James. The Professor was much older than he was, but had shown Nigel respect from the time he'd been young. Nigel had always been ruthless and ambitious, even as a boy. He liked to think that his older cousin had recognized him as a kindred spirit. There may have been another reason too. Maybe Professor Moriarity knew that, given enough time, Nigel might become even more evil than he was, and it would be better to have him as a friend than as an enemy.

Nigel smiled to himself. He followed the workers and the explosives into the huge mechanical lift he'd designed and pulled the switch that initiated their ascent. As the lift rose directly beneath a secret entrance in the clock tower, he removed a folded piece of paper from his jacket pocket. His eyes darted over the copy of Frederick Dent's plans, checking the placement of his electronics and the explosives. He couldn't afford to miss a single flaw in his diabolical scheme.

But he couldn't find a one. Not one. It was perfect.

THE CHASE

*B*OOOM! Thunder echoed around Griffin as the steam engine roared to life. Then the same piercing whistle they had heard before blew from a hidden area on the train, giving Griffin goose bumps. Suddenly the train lurched forward and rocketed down the tracks.

Griffin had never traveled so fast in his life. The cavern walls passed by in a blur, and he gripped the seat in front of him with white-knuckled terror. He was somewhere between complete exhilaration and total panic!

"I say, Snodgrass! Slow this thing down!" shouted Mr. Dent. But Snodgrass, who sat in the seat in front of them, didn't respond. He was so busy pulling cranks, watching gauges, and twisting switches that he didn't have time to speak.

With the wind blasting through his hair, Griffin inched forward and leaned over the seat so that he could see better what his uncle was doing. He saw a gauge marked Water Pressure and noticed that the indicator arrow was all the way up into the red. Snodgrass was focused on the gauge, trying to lower the pressure.

But whether the switch was broken or the machine only had one setting was impossible to say. The tracks flew under the churning wheels, the wind whistled fiercely around them, and the engine shuddered to the point that Griffin felt certain if they didn't slow down soon, it was sure to fall apart.

The train suddenly rocketed upward, climbing an impossibly steep mountainside of track. Then, with a resounding *WHOOSH!* the engine burst above ground. Griffin gasped, taking the first breath of fresh air he'd had in hours.

The sun blazed overhead, and the train, showing no signs of slowing, headed straight toward Charring Cross Station. As the train picked up speed on the straightaway, Snodgrass fumbled desperately at the controls, searching for a brake. Other trains were making their way toward the station, and Griffin could see people gawking and pointing at their incredibly fast-moving engine.

Then Griffin realized they weren't just pointing at them. On the same track coming toward them was another train!

"Uncle, look out!" Griffin shouted.

Snodgrass glanced up from the control box just in time to see the fast-approaching train. The big engine's whistle bellowed as the two of them sped on a collision course.

"I can't locate the brake!" Snodgrass shouted.

Griffin's eyes darted around the cockpit, looking for any lever he could find. The blast of the approaching train's whistle grew louder. Suddenly he spotted a brass knob on the floor near his uncle's foot.

"Down there! By your foot! Is that it?" he shouted at Snodgrass.

His uncle looked to where his nephew was pointing.

The big freight train was so close that Griffin could make out the pale face of the other engineer shouting with fright.

Snodgrass stomped on the button.

It wasn't a brake.

Instead, just as their engine was about to crash, they switched tracks. The button, without any appearance of wires, had operated a railroad switch! The other train rocketed by, almost close enough for Griffin to reach out and touch its speeding cars.

Seconds later Charring Cross station was nothing but a speck behind them, and the tracks ahead looked clear. Griffin breathed a huge sigh and wiped his sweating brow.

But he didn't have time to relax. For then, just as he collapsed backward into his seat, rivets suddenly started popping off the front of the train. Griffin watched with horror as a huge piece of smokestack suddenly flew off and went bouncing down the tracks behind them.

"It's falling apart!" he screamed.

Snodgrass turned to Griffin. The wind was howling so loudly around them that he had to shout in Griffin's ear to be heard. "Take the controls!"

"But I don't know how," Griffin protested. "What about Mr. Dent?"

Snodgrass pointed. The boy turned around and saw that Frederick Dent had fainted.

Trembling from head to foot, Griffin climbed over the back of his uncle's seat and gripped the control handle. Snodgrass, fighting against the terrible winds, climbed out onto the front of the engine with a hammer gripped in his hand.

Terrified, Griffin began to pray, begging God to show them

mercy and to somehow rescue them from what looked like a terrible fate. He glanced down at the gauges and noticed that the one that said Water Pressure had gotten so high its measuring needle had broken off.

Faster and faster their engine sped along. It was no wonder that Moriarty hadn't wanted to use it; the thing seemed to possess a mind of its own and didn't respond to any of the controls!

Perched on the front of the train, Snodgrass pounded as many of the rivets as he could back into the metal, desperately trying to keep the train from flying apart. Griffin's eyes flicked over all the controls, searching for anything that might help him find a way to stop.

Glancing up, Griffin saw Westminster Palace suddenly looming in front of them. His quick eye also observed that about a hundred feet ahead of them, almost paralleling the track they were on, was a spur of track that looked newly made. Someone had clearly tried to conceal it, but the passage of the first train must have made it more visible.

Whether it was instinct or Providence, Griffin knew that it was important that they switch over. Without consulting his uncle, Griffin punched the button on the floor with his shoe. Like before, the speeding engine suddenly jumped tracks. And the next thing they knew, they were shooting back down under the earth, going down a set of tracks that led inside a tunnel.

Everything was pitch-black.

All Griffin could hear was the howl of the wind on either side of him and his uncle's furious pounding on the metal casing.

Please, Lord, Griffin prayed, *help me find a way to stop this train.*

He couldn't have said why he didn't see it before. Perhaps it was because the world around him had just been plunged into total darkness, but Griffin noticed for the first time that a tiny electric light pulsed in a tight compartment next to his seat. Griffin had only seen an Edison electric bulb once before, when his father had taken him to Menlo Park on a family vacation. At that time, he'd thought it the most wonderful invention in the world.

But now, as he could see what this tiny bulb illuminated, his gratitude to Mr. Edison for his invention doubled. For there, next to his seat, was a handle marked Emergency Brake.

Griffin shouted to his uncle, "I found it!"

A light appeared at the end of the tunnel. Looking ahead, Griffin could see an underground station and the outline of an engine very like the one he was in stopped on the tracks ahead.

Snodgrass must have seen it too. As he leapt back into the compartment beside Griffin, the boy pulled back on the emergency brake lever as hard as he could.

Sparks flew from behind the churning metal wheels, covering the tunnel walls with dancing light. A scraping sound pitched so high that it made Griffin's hair stand on end echoed in the tunnel all around them. Griffin found that he was yelling, his mouth wide-open in a terrified scream that seemed to pitch itself to the same piercing note as the screeching wheels.

The other engine drew impossibly close. There was no way they would stop in time! Frederick Dent awoke from his faint just as the back end of a train rushed toward them.

His eyes flew open, and he threw his arms over his face.

THE CLOCK TOWER

But then, just as they were about to impact the back end of the other train, they stopped. And Griffin, pale and shaky, practically melted into the engine's floorboards with relief.

"A little close," commented Snodgrass. Griffin saw how badly his uncle's hand shook as he ran his hand through his disheveled hair. Griffin looked back and saw that Frederick Dent, once again, had fainted.

"What time is it?" demanded Griffin. Snodgrass checked his pocket watch.

"Eleven fifteen a.m."

They didn't have a single second to waste. At twelve o'clock the bomb was going to explode!

"We've got to stop them!" Griffin shouted as he ran down the side of tracks toward the metal lift. Snodgrass paused only to retrieve his electric spear from the cab of the train and then followed.

"We'll have to come back for Dent," Snodgrass said bitterly. "It's his own fault for passing out at a time like this."

Griffin hated to leave him behind. He was worried that Dent would be kidnapped again if the criminals returned. At the very least they would want to stop Dent from going to Scotland Yard with what he knew. Of course, by then it would be far too late. And since he'd already served his purpose, Griffin could only hope that the clockmaker held no further interest for Moriarty.

Griffin reached the lift first and pulled the lever to bring the platform to their level. He waited impatiently and hopped on as soon as the lift touched the ground, his uncle right behind him. Then he pulled the switch again, and they began to rise up out of the makeshift train station. It moved much more slowly than he'd hoped, and he found himself doing random math equations in his head in an effort to try to calm down.

After what seemed like an eternity, the lift stopped and they were able to open the heavy door. To Griffin's amazement, they found themselves inside the gigantic clock tower, staring upward at the mammoth gears.

"Time?" asked Griffin.

"Eleven twenty-six," Snodgrass replied.

Now that they were here, Griffin had absolutely no idea what to do next. He'd gotten them within striking distance, but didn't know how to stop the villains or their clock bomb. Running a hand down to his hip, he was comforted to find the Stinger still there in its holster. He gazed around the interior of the clock, searching for a way to go farther up. Then he spotted the twisting staircase that was bolted to the side of a nearby wall and instinctively knew that what he was looking for would probably be at the top.

Griffin dashed toward the staircase and began to climb. Snodgrass followed, his electric spear firmly in his grip. Griffin counted as he climbed, and when he reached the top, hitting stair three hundred thirty-two, his legs felt like rubber.

There was a platform with a window at the top, and Griffin wobbled over to it and looked down. Far below, he could see a courtyard decorated for the ceremony that would honor Sherlock Holmes. Hansom cabs were lined up, and one, possibly the royal coach, was headed toward a throne positioned near the stage.

"Uncle," Griffin gasped. "What time is it?"

Snodgrass, breathing hard, checked his watch. "Eleven forty."

Griffin looked wildly around and noticed a heavy door off to one side. He rushed over and threw it open. Before him was a huge room filled with gears and a swinging pendulum. Loud ticking, like a heartbeat, filled the chamber. And standing there, surrounded by his henchmen with the gigantic glass clock face behind them, was someone he recognized.

Quickly filing through several photographs in his mind, Griffin searched his memory to find out where he'd seen his face before. But it didn't take him too long to figure it out. It was the friendly conductor he'd met on the train when he'd first arrived in London. The man wore the same pince-nez glasses and had the same curled moustache.

But he realized that the man he was looking at was not simply a train conductor. He was Moriarty. Griffin knew he had made a terrible mistake when he'd assumed that Moriarty's sleeves were dirty because of coal.

"Well, well, well. If it isn't the nephew of the great

detective!" Moriarty exclaimed as he noticed Griffin. "Now you've ridden on my trains twice. Tell me, did you prefer the first or the second?"

"It wasn't coal on your sleeves that day we met, was it? It was gunpowder," Griffin said softly.

"That is correct. I was posing as a conductor in order to study the tracks and time the arrival of the trains that led to Charring Cross station. Earlier I had been moving the explosives and forgot to change my shirt. Too bad you didn't figure it out sooner," said Moriarty.

Griffin noted that any hint of the friendly demeanor he'd seen when he first encountered the man was completely gone.

Moriarty's lip twisted in a sneer as he said, "How has your visit been with your uncle, Sherlock Holmes?" Then, turning to Snodgrass, he said, "But who is this, then? Surely it can't be the great detective?"

"Only someone as cruel as you could think up a scheme like this," said Snodgrass. "And I should have guessed sooner that you were related to the Professor."

Griffin looked up at his uncle, feeling puzzled. "You mean this isn't Professor Moriarty?"

"No, Griffin. This is Nigel Moriarty, a person for whom I've been searching for many years."

Then Griffin realized the truth. Nigel Moriarty was the same "Nigel" who had attacked his uncle and his mother when they were children and had tortured Snoops.

A look of disgust flickered across Griffin's face as he stared back at the man on the platform. Moriarty didn't notice. He was looking at Snodgrass, recognition dawning on him at last.

"Well, well, if it isn't my old school chum, 'Sniveling'

Snodgrass." Moriarty cackled. His thugs joined in, guffawing loudly.

Moriarty strode closer to where they stood, his silver-topped cane swinging as he walked. "I remember enjoying playing with your dog. What did you call him? Snoops?" He registered the tightening on Snodgrass's face. "Yes," he murmured, "that was the name, wasn't it?"

Then, moving within inches of Snodgrass's face, he said, "You know, the trouble with basset hounds is that they have very sensitive ears. You might want to try a different breed next time. One that isn't so weak—"

Snodgrass lashed out with his spear with such speed that Moriarty was nearly caught off guard. However, he managed to dodge the blow at the last second and with a deft motion unsheathed a hidden sword from inside his cane.

Griffin pulled the Stinger from his holster and began firing at the crowd of thugs. While engaged in combat, his eyes darted constantly to the rows of ticking gears, searching. He couldn't see any explosives, though he assumed they were hidden somewhere inside the giant clock. But that was not what he was looking for.

Somewhere inside the clock there had to be a switch that, when the clock struck twelve, would trigger the explosives. As he fought, shooting indiscriminately at the approaching thugs, he searched desperately for any sign of the device.

Before he even realized it, Griffin had dispatched three of the henchmen, blasting them with glowing plasma and sending them into a deep sleep. Three remained, and even though they seemed pretty stupid, they had seen what Griffin's weapon could do and were making it difficult for him to get a clear shot.

The thugs drew long knives and hid behind the gigantic gears, waiting for an opportunity to strike. Meanwhile, Snodgrass and Moriarty were engaged in combat, with the gigantic hands of the clock in silhouette behind them.

The hands were positioned at five minutes to twelve. Snodgrass swung with his spear and Moriarty parried, sending Griffin's uncle reeling backward. The butt end of his spear crashed through the massive clock face, sending shards of glass hurtling toward the Palace and ceremony below.

The tinkle of that falling glass alerted the ever-watchful Holmes to the situation. The tall detective was sitting on a velvet-lined chair, listening to Her Royal Highness talk about his illustrious career and his service to the Crown. But when the shards of glass hit the earth, his head jerked up, like a bloodhound catching wind of a scent.

It didn't take more than a moment for him to realize that something was going on behind the giant clock face of Big Ben. The detective's keen gaze saw the tiny shadows at the top of the tower and, after a quick apology to the Queen and the audience, leapt into action.

It was 11:57. They were almost out of time.

A knife whizzed by the side of Griffin's head, narrowly missing his ear. He returned fire at the thug who had thrown it, but missed. His eyes flicked desperately around the room, searching . . . searching.

And then he saw it. Set deep between rows of turning gears was a small, black box. It was almost completely obscured by the clockworks, and getting to it looked nearly impossible. How Moriarty had managed to hide it there was beyond Griffin's powers of imagination.

The giant minute hands clunked forward.

Eleven fifty-eight.

Please, God, show me what to— But before he'd even finished his prayer, the solution presented itself. It was a terribly desperate thing to do, and yet Griffin knew that even if it cost him his life, it was worth saving the lives of others.

He rushed up to where Snodgrass and Moriarty were fighting. The battle seemed to be nearly over. Moriarty towered over his uncle, his sword pointed triumphantly at his chest. Griffin saw that his uncle's spear was lying nearby, out of reach.

Moriarty glanced at the giant hands of the clock and back down to Snodgrass. Without saying a word, Griffin knew what he was thinking.

They were all doomed.

There wasn't enough time to escape the blast. But judging by the look on the villain's face, he was going to kill Snodgrass before being killed himself, if only for the pleasure of seeing him die.

Knives flew past Griffin as he ran toward his uncle. He was so intent upon his plan that he didn't see one of Moriarty's henchman coming toward him with his long, glittering blade out and ready. The scarred man's face was twisted with animal ferocity, and when he threw the blade, it flew with deadly accuracy.

Griffin felt a pinch on his calf. One of the knives must have nicked him. But he ignored it, took aim at Moriarty, and fired.

The Stinger's blast narrowly missed the villain, but it did knock Moriarty off balance. Hoping that it had bought his uncle an advantage, Griffin knelt, dropped the Stinger, and grabbed his uncle's electrical spear.

Eleven fifty-nine.

Griffin tried to run back toward the giant gears, but suddenly realized that his leg wasn't working. Looking down, he saw a crimson pool gathering around his shoe. The last knife hadn't just nicked him. Numbly, he looked at the knife handle that protruded out of the side of his calf and the vast amount of blood on the floor.

Fighting for every ounce of strength, he limped as close as he could to the rotating gears. There was no sign of Moriarty's thugs anywhere. Apparently they'd fled the clock tower, anxious to save their own lives.

Griffin could sense that there was no time left, that at any moment the gigantic minute hand would swing into place and the clock would strike twelve. His leg was throbbing as the shock wore off, and he felt dizzy, his vision cloudy from the loss of blood.

He'd only have one chance, a single shot to hit the box.

He thought desperately of David when he faced Goliath. In that story, a young boy had brought down a giant in one shot. And Griffin knew that his hand had been guided by the Lord.

As You helped David, please, help me now . . .

Griffin pulled the trigger on the spear, and as the electricity sparked, he threw the spear toward the box with all of his might.

But he never saw whether or not the spear hit the target. Suddenly he felt a terrible pain and, looking down, saw the point of Moriarty's sword protruding from the middle of his chest. Then everything went black.

Griffin was already unconscious when Snodgrass shot Moriarty in the back with the Stinger, sending him into a coma-like sleep to wait for police. But after shooting the villain, Snodgrass didn't watch as Moriarty slumped to the floor. Nor was he aware that as the gigantic hands of the clock swung into place, the clock struck the twelve o'clock hour without an explosion.

Rupert Snodgrass rushed to his nephew's side and gathered Griffin's lifeless body into his arms and wept. Nigel Moriarty had already stolen someone he'd cared deeply about once before, and now it had happened again. And it was more painful than he could have ever imagined.

Snodgrass barely felt the consoling hand that touched his shoulder. His eyes were so blurred with tears that he didn't recognize Sherlock Holmes, who had arrived at the scene of the crime too late for once.

There was no triumph for Rupert Snodgrass. Even if he'd

been able to see Holmes, to know that he'd finally beaten the Great Detective in solving a case before he had, he wouldn't have cared. All that mattered now was his nephew.

And it seemed like Griffin was gone forever.

RECOVERY

For many days Griffin was lost somewhere between waking and sleeping. He was dimly aware of throbbing pain in his chest and calf, white-shirted doctors, the smell of iodine, and the whirr of machinery as it pumped up and down around him.

But eventually, he did awake. And when he did, the first person he saw sitting beside his bed was his uncle.

Rupert Snodgrass was asleep, slumped in a chair. His arm was in a sling, and Griffin was surprised that he was dressed differently than when he'd last seen him. He wore a clean suit and had even shaved! And in spite of being groggy, Griffin's keen gaze also noticed that while shaving he'd missed twelve whiskers, that a bit of shaving cream had dried behind his ear, and that his collar had been put on upside down. But for all of his finery, his uncle looked very tired. There were dark circles beneath his eyes, and Griffin noticed new lines on his haggard face.

Griffin turned his gaze around the room and felt disoriented. How much time had passed since he'd been in the clock tower?

His uncle must have heard him stir, because his eyes flicked open. He gazed at Griffin for a moment as if having a hard time believing what he was seeing. Then he exhaled slowly, as if he'd been holding his breath for a long time. He moved to Griffin's bedside and, smiling, awkwardly patted his shoulder.

"Welcome to the waking world, Griffin."

"How long have I been asleep?" Griffin asked. He was surprised to hear how weak his voice sounded.

"Five days," said his uncle. "For a while there, the doctors weren't sure that you were going to stay with us."

"Is he awake?" a voice said. Griffin looked up and saw a priest enter the room. The man was small, elderly, and had a friendly face. He took one look at Griffin and clasped his hands together.

"Well, God be praised," the priest said happily. Then he turned to Snodgrass and said, "Do you see, Rupert? Our prayers have been answered!"

Griffin gave his uncle a surprised look. Snodgrass cleared his throat awkwardly and looked away.

"Well, my boy, it looks as if you've had quite an adventure! The entire city owes you and your uncle a great debt," said the priest.

Suddenly all the images from their crazy train ride and battle at the clock tower rushed back to Griffin. Obviously, since he was still alive, the last-minute shot he'd made with his uncle's electric spear must have hit its target.

Snodgrass, seeming to read his thoughts, explained, "How you ever conceived of such a stroke of genius as to throw the spear into the bomb's triggering mechanism I'll never guess," he said warmly. "It was magnificent to watch the sparks fly as the box shorted out, and even more to see the expression on Nigel Moriarty's face as he realized his plan was foiled."

"Did they take him to prison?" Griffin asked.

"Well, er, there was a problem," Snodgrass said grimly. He sighed and shrugged his shoulders. "Moriarty's ability to elude justice is legendary. The night after he was delivered to his jail cell, there was an escape. The officers believe that one of their own was in on it."

Griffin winced. It would have made him feel much better to know that such an evil man was behind bars, where he could never hurt anyone again.

"But there is good news. Her Royal Highness was very generous in her praise and reward. She's had her personal doctors attending you. And I can assure you that you will never again have to eat dried kippers and blood sausage if you don't want to."

Griffin smiled. They had succeeded in solving the mystery and saving the Queen, and now his uncle wouldn't have to worry about being evicted from his flat either! If only Moriarty were behind bars, things would have been perfect.

Griffin tried to turn over and noticed a sudden, shooting pain in his leg. He groaned and clenched his teeth.

"You must be careful, boy," Snodgrass said. Then his expression grew troubled. "I'm afraid your leg won't be what it used to be."

Griffin stared up at his uncle's anxious face. He felt a surge of panic.

"What do you mean? Will I be able to walk? To run? Will it get better with more time?"

"The doctors say that you will walk again," said the priest consolingly. "But it will probably be with a limp." He moved closer to Griffin's bedside and laid his hand upon Griffin's wrist.

"I know that is crushing news for a boy your age. But everything happens for a reason. And I know God has a great plan for a brave boy like you. Your uncle has told me of your great faith, son. I would encourage you to remember the story of Jacob as he wrestled with the angel. Do you remember that one?"

Griffin nodded, and the priest smiled gently. "The Book says that Jacob walked with a limp after that great struggle. Although the Scriptures don't elaborate further, I like to think that for Jacob that limp was a reminder that God had touched him personally. He'd chosen him to do something truly great."

Griffin stared at the kindly priest, trying his best to be brave. The words were encouraging, but it was hard to accept that he would never run again. But he was alive, and he had saved hundreds of lives, including the Queen's. God was good. And if all he had was a limp to show for the incredible danger he'd been through, then he had reason to be thankful.

"Thank you. I'll try to remember that," Griffin said, smiling at the kind old man.

"Well, I have some other patients to attend to," said the priest. "Get some rest, young man. You've certainly earned it!"

"Thank you, Father Brown," said Snodgrass, shaking his hand. The little priest smiled as he left the room.

Looking down, Griffin realized that the priest had left a small Bible next to him on the bed. He flipped to the New Testament and held it comfortingly. After a moment, he glanced at his uncle and gave him a smile.

"So, am I to understand that you were actually praying for my recovery?" Griffin asked. Then, with his eyes twinkling, added, "I'm just curious. To whom were those prayers directed,

Uncle? I thought you said something about not believing in gods of any kind."

Snodgrass looked away and coughed. Griffin heard him mutter, "Coincidence," under his breath.

They laughed.

28

221B

The following week Griffin was allowed to return to his uncle's house. His chest was much better. Luckily, the sword hadn't hit any organs, so that wound had healed quickly. His leg hadn't done as well. It was still tender, but was healing as best it could. As the cab pulled up to 221 Baker Street, Griffin felt a powerful sense of relief. His uncle helped him disembark, and with the use of a small cane, he was able to navigate his way up the now familiar staircase that led to his uncle's flat.

Upon entering the foyer, Griffin was surprised to see Watts standing there. Snodgrass hurried in behind Griffin and said, "I've, er, modified Watts's settings. From now on, he'll answer to your commands just the same as mine. I've instructed him to make you comfortable, so make sure you tell him anything you might need. He's actually quite good at chess, if you feel like playing."

Griffin smiled up at his uncle. "Thank you."

Rupert gave him a quick pat on the back and then said in a gruff voice, "Watts, help this boy up to the sofa. He needs rest."

"Yes, sir," came the robot's mechanical voice.

With his uncle on one side and the robot on the other, Griffin was helped down the hallway and into the parlor. Griffin gazed around in amazement. The entire area was clean! His uncle's inventions still decorated the walls, but instead of lying haphazardly around the room, they were neatly put away on shelves or in corners.

The sofa was piled high with pillows and an afghan, and Griffin climbed up onto it and made himself comfortable. He couldn't believe the change that had occurred since he'd been gone.

Snodgrass noticed Griffin's amazement and replied, "I had Watts straighten up a bit. You'll need a place to recover, and I thought staying in your bedroom might get to be a bit boring. This way you'll have two comfortable spots."

When he had first arrived, Griffin had been instructed to never enter his uncle's workroom. And now Snodgrass was giving it up so that he could rest. He was reminded that with God's help, and by extending love and kindness to someone, anything was possible.

Watts disappeared into the kitchen and returned shortly bearing a silver tray in his mechanical arms. Piled high upon it were scones from Tottingham's bakery along with a steaming pot of tea.

The journey from the hospital had taxed Griffin's strength, and the smell of the flaky pastries made his stomach growl loudly. He ate one of the delicious scones and let out a sigh while his uncle went to answer a knock at the door. Things had definitely improved for the better at his uncle's house.

Snodgrass reappeared a few minutes later with a startled look on his face.

"What is it?" Griffin asked, sipping his tea.

His uncle paused before answering. Then, holding up a small, white envelope, he said, "It's a letter from Sherlock Holmes. He . . . he's invited us over for tea."

Griffin's jaw dropped, and he nearly spilled his tea. "But why?"

"I think it's time I tell you the whole story of what happened in the tower," Snodgrass said, sitting on the edge of the sofa. "Mr. Holmes showed up right after you were stabbed. He'd been following the case, but didn't figure out what was going on until some of the shattered glass from the clock hit the ground. It was only then he knew what the Moriartys had planned."

Griffin must have looked as confused as he felt, because his uncle laughed and patted his shoulder.

"Well, he was bound to show up sooner or later. There's hardly anything that goes on in London that escapes his attention. He recognized Nigel Moriarty immediately, of course, and did everything he could to secure that scoundrel for the police. But he was even more helpful with you. He knew just what to do to help your wounds," Snodgrass said.

Griffin was flattered that the great detective had taken an interest in him. "What happened next?" he asked.

"We carried you back down the stairs and took you to the hospital. After that, I spoke to Scotland Yard about everything that had happened. It wasn't long before they discovered where Moriarty had hidden all of the explosives."

"I was wondering about that," said Griffin. "Where were they?"

"It was ingenious," said Snodgrass. "They were in plain sight. Moriarty had painted them to look like they were part of the decor inside the clock tower."

Griffin thought about the incredibly detailed seagull camera and the beautiful steam engine. He hated to admit it, but Nigel Moriarty was a very accomplished artist! Only someone that talented could have hidden something so deadly in plain sight. Griffin thought that it was a shame that Moriarty used that God-given talent for evil instead of good.

Snodgrass continued, "Holmes and the police were flabbergasted when I explained everything to them. They were especially amazed by those special trains. I believe that since their discovery, they've been declared the official property of the British government. Hopefully they can take the design and use it to improve the railway system."

They were silent for a moment. Griffin thought about all the incredible things that had happened during their adventure and was amazed that he'd come out of it all alive. He'd never felt so proud of himself before. This hadn't been a test in school or a spelling bee; Griffin had actually made a difference in the world. Not only that, but they had somehow solved the crime without the help of London's greatest detective, Sherlock Holmes!

Griffin wondered how his uncle felt about Holmes now that he had finally bested the great detective. He was excited by the prospect of actually meeting their neighbor; however, he wanted to be sensitive to his uncle's feelings and said, "I suppose we could refuse Sherlock Holmes's invitation for tea. That is, I'm sure we have a lot of work to do with the police, filling out paperwork and telling them all about the case. I'm sure Mr. Holmes would understand."

But Snodgrass surprised him. His uncle folded the letter and with a resolute expression said, "No, it would be rude not to attend. I think we should clean up a bit and then go next door and see what Sherlock Holmes has to say. After all, it wouldn't be neighborly to refuse."

Things had certainly changed in the past few weeks!

Watts helped Griffin dress and comb his hair. He was still having a hard time getting used to his uncooperative leg, and it would take a little time before he regained total self-reliance.

A few minutes later Griffin and his uncle were standing at the entrance to 221B. Snodgrass was dressed in a brand-new tweed jacket and was wearing, of all things, a very loud and obnoxious tie.

He noticed Griffin's stare and mentioned that it was very expensive and fashionable. Griffin suppressed a snicker just as the door swung open and Mrs. Hudson, Sherlock Holmes's landlady, appeared in the doorway.

"Do come in, gentlemen," she said, and then added to his uncle, "I received the check for the rent yesterday. I'm looking forward to it becoming a regular habit."

"That is my intention, Mrs. Hudson," Griffin's uncle said. "I feel certain that I won't have to impose upon your generous nature in the future."

Griffin noticed that she had a kindly face, but could tell by her manner that she had a no-nonsense side. From what he'd read in the stories, she wasn't even afraid of Sherlock Holmes.

Griffin followed his uncle. They were shown into the

famous detective's sitting room. Griffin tried to suppress his excitement as he saw Sherlock Holmes for the first time. The great detective was sitting in a wing-backed chair, clad in a blue robe and smoking a pipe. On the sofa opposite was the esteemed Dr. Watson with his sandy hair and bushy mustache. Watson smiled at Griffin as he entered and, noticing his limp, helped escort him to a nearby chair.

"Gentlemen," said Holmes, "I'm happy that you decided to accept my offer."

Griffin noticed that Sherlock Holmes had a quick, clipped method of speaking. It was almost as if the words themselves were chosen because they were precise rather than poetic. He gave Griffin a vague, appraising look.

"You seem to be healing nicely, young man," Holmes said. "And if you continue eating Mrs. Tottingham's excellent scones, I'm sure you'll put some much-needed meat on your bones."

Griffin wasn't startled in the least by Holmes's observation. Looking down, he noticed the three tiny crumbs on his collar and grinned.

"Thank you, sir," he said. "I shall endeavor to eat more carefully next time."

To Griffin's surprise, Holmes chuckled. Turning to Watson, he said, "I see we have an observant boy here, Watson. It's a rare occurrence when my initial deductions don't surprise a newcomer."

He nodded to Griffin approvingly, and the boy felt a surge of pleasure. *A compliment from Sherlock Holmes!* What would his parents say to that?

But while Griffin was feeling at ease in the presence of the famous detective, his uncle was obviously not. Snodgrass sat politely, but Griffin could see a slight scowl on his uncle's face. He knew that it was hard for him to be there and that he was doing it purely to be polite.

Somehow Griffin felt certain that Holmes was aware of this, but he didn't say anything. Mrs. Hudson brought out a tray with a pot of tea, and Griffin was surprised to see that it was laden with some of the same pastries he had enjoyed from Mrs. Tottingham's earlier that day.

Evidently he and Sherlock Holmes shared similar tastes!

After they'd each been given a cup of tea and something to munch on, Sherlock Holmes stood from his chair and leaned against the mantel by the fire. He puffed on his pipe for a couple of seconds and then, turning to Griffin's uncle, said, "I'm afraid I owe you an apology, Mr. Snodgrass."

Griffin saw his uncle's eyes widen with surprise.

"I'm afraid I don't understand," he said haltingly.

Holmes paused for a moment and then said in a voice much different than his normal, clipped tone, "You must have thought me quite heartless, to have never helped you when you came to me all those years ago about your missing dog."

Snodgrass's eyes narrowed. Griffin could tell that he hadn't expected this.

"The fact is, as Dr. Watson can attest, there aren't many cases that I've been unable to solve. And it was pride that kept me from admitting that yours was one of those cases. Pride, and an unwillingness to tell a small boy that the greatest detective in London couldn't find his best friend."

Griffin couldn't read his uncle's thoughts, but the news was definitely a shock. He noticed that his uncle's hands trembled with suppressed emotion.

Holmes continued, sounding genuinely sorry. "If it is of any consolation, I never did give up searching. In the end, I found a farmer in the northern country who described a hound very much like the one you had. And that dog sired a pup, which has proved very useful to me on many occasions."

Holmes motioned to Mrs. Hudson, who disappeared down the hallway. She returned a moment later with a friendly looking basset hound. When Rupert Snodgrass saw the dog, his mouth fell open in surprise. It had the same silver star on its forehead that Snodgrass had described Snoops as having had.

"Mr. Snodgrass, this is Toby. And he's the best nose in London, just like his father before him. I would like it very much if you would please accept him as a gift."

Snodgrass was speechless. Toby moved over to Rupert's knee and laid his head upon it, his tail wagging and waiting to be patted on the head. Snodgrass raised a trembling hand and gently stroked the hound's forehead. The look that Griffin saw on his uncle's face made his eyes fill with tears.

Holmes politely looked away, not wanting either of his guests to feel embarrassed. "One of the reasons that I asked you to tea was to let you know that there is going to be a change here at Baker Street."

Griffin looked up, wondering what Holmes was getting at. The detective glanced at Mrs. Hudson, who was standing in the doorway, sniffing and dabbing at her eyes with a handkerchief.

"What I'm trying to say is that I'm going to retire. I am moving to Sussex Downs and looking forward to a quiet life as a beekeeper."

For the first time, Griffin noticed just how old Sherlock Holmes was. In the illustrations in the *Strand Magazine*, he was always depicted as a fairly young and energetic man. But although he still seemed very fit and alert, Griffin could detect traces of silver in his hair and fine wrinkles around his eyes.

Holmes continued, saying, "If there is anything I can ever do for either of you, you have but to ask. For I can honestly say, I owe you my life. And judging by your superb performance at the clock tower, I feel absolutely certain that Baker Street is being left in very capable hands." He offered them an elegant bow.

Now it was Griffin's turn to be speechless. He felt honored and amazed that Holmes would bestow such incredible praise. He glanced at his uncle, whose demeanor had completely changed. All of the years of hard resentment had disappeared from his face. He looked like a man transformed.

Snodgrass rose from where he was sitting and walked over to Holmes and extended his hand. Holmes shook it, and the two shared a smile.

Watson interrupted, speaking for the first time. In his gentle, deep voice he asked, "Mr. Snodgrass, if it wouldn't be too much trouble, I would love to hear a detailed account of what happened to you and your nephew at the clock tower. As you probably know, I write about my friend Holmes for the *Strand Magazine*. Since he's retiring, would you mind if I wrote down one of your adventures as a supplement? I'm not boasting when I say that nearly every person in England reads the magazine, and you will be made famous overnight!"

Snodgrass looked at Watson and smiled. Then he moved next to Griffin and put his arm around his nephew's shoulders.

Griffin's heart leapt with joy.

His uncle had finally been presented with everything

he had ever wanted. Not only had he beat the great Sherlock Holmes in solving a mystery that had saved England, but now he was being offered a chance to get all the fame and publicity that his rival had enjoyed for years. For him, it had to be a dream come true.

But Griffin was surprised when he heard his uncle say instead, "Thank you, Dr. Watson. I am quite overcome by your generous offer. However, I think that my nephew and I would prefer anonymity. It will be far easier for the two of us to solve crimes if the criminals don't know who we are or see us coming. Isn't that right, Griffin?"

Snodgrass looked down at Griffin and smiled. Griffin couldn't believe what he had heard. Griffin had never desired fame of any kind, and it made a lot of sense to keep a low profile as a private investigator. It was just shocking that uncle Rupert had turned it down! In the weeks that he'd spent with his uncle, it had seemed like this was all he'd ever wanted. But the thing that really amazed Griffin was that, for the first time, his uncle had treated him as if they were a detective team.

As equals.

His prayers had been answered. Not only was he getting to put his talents to use, but he'd also found in his uncle a true friend.

"Yes, Uncle, I think that would be just fine," Griffin replied in a husky voice. He was so happy he felt that he could have exploded right there on the spot!

As they made ready to go back to their apartment, Holmes stopped Griffin.

"Mr. Sharpe, I have something for you as well," he said, handing Griffin a slim cane with a silver tip.

It was Nigel Moriarty's cane. With a sick feeling, Griffin knew that hidden within it was the same sword that had given him his chest wound.

"I've noticed that your encounter with Nigel Moriarty has left an indelible impression," Holmes said, nodding in the direction of Griffin's hurt leg. "And I think that perhaps a walking stick might make moving around easier. As it happens, this one was abandoned by its owner in the clock-tower."

Griffin took the cane, but he wasn't sure he could use it. It felt strange to carry the weapon that had almost killed him.

Holmes continued, "Young man, we share some of the same qualities of observation. And I can say without hesitation that you bear upon you the makings of a great detective." Holmes gave Griffin a serious look. "So perhaps that walking stick will serve to remind you that your enemy is still out there and that you should remain vigilant. For the criminal mind never sleeps, Mr. Sharpe. And neither should yours."

Griffin studied the dark cane with its silver handle. Looking closer, he saw the initials N.M. etched into its surface. He lowered the cane to the ground, and although it was a little bit tall for him, he leaned upon it experimentally.

It supported him nicely.

Griffin nodded his thanks and shook hands with the greatest detective the world had ever seen. And then, with his new walking stick in hand, he exited the apartment, walking taller than he ever had in his life.

GOING HOME

It was late August. Griffin packed his suitcase, one much nicer than the one he'd arrived with.

The summer he'd spent with his uncle had proved to be one of the most exciting he'd ever had. After the Clock Tower Mystery, they'd had several other cases together, and so many had come through their door that Griffin had even had to solve a few completely on his own!

He was sad to leave. Over the last few months, the apartment on Baker Street had truly become his home. He missed his parents, and he was very excited to see them. But he'd also found family here in London, and he knew that he would miss his uncle terribly. Part of him wished he could stay in England and finish school here, but he was sure his parents would never agree to that.

Down the hall, Toby barked, his signal to Watts that someone was at the door. The robot had been modified to recognize the hound's bark and marched over to greet the visitors. Griffin swung off of his bed and, with his trusty stick in hand, limped carefully down the hall.

Mr. and Mrs. Dent were standing in the entryway. When they caught sight of Griffin, they smiled.

"Hello, young man!" Mrs. Dent said. And, to his surprise, she embraced him in a warm hug. Griffin smiled too. It was so good to see her happy again.

Snodgrass entered, wiping his hands on a towel. Griffin could tell that he'd been working on his latest invention, the Chrono-Teleporter. It was truly shaping up to be an amazing device, possibly his uncle's greatest invention. When he'd told him about it, Griffin had been amused to hear that it didn't have "Snodgrass" in its title at all.

"Mr. and Mrs. Dent! This is a surprise," said Snodgrass warmly. "What can we do for you?"

Mr. Dent beamed at the detective. "We felt that we never had a chance to thank you properly and wanted to express just how much we appreciate what you've done for us."

He removed two small packages from his pocket and handed one to Rupert and one to Griffin. "It's a small token of my esteem, a trifle really," said Mr. Dent.

Mrs. Dent interrupted, "Don't be ridiculous, Frederick." She turned to Griffin and his uncle and said, "My husband is being modest. He has been working on those for several weeks. You'll find that they are truly remarkable and, in my opinion, some of his very best work."

Griffin opened the box and saw glittering there a beautiful gold pocket watch. Lifting the watch, he saw etched on its outer surface a perfect illustration of Big Ben, and as he opened the lid, "Westminster Chimes" tinkled gently from its hidden depths.

It was beautiful—a true work of art.

"Mr. Dent, I don't know what to say," Snodgrass said. Griffin glanced at his uncle and saw that he was as overcome with the Dents' generosity as he was.

Mr. Dent beamed. "A simple thank you will more than suffice. I owe you gentlemen everything." He looked at Mrs. Dent and gave her shoulders a quick squeeze. "You not only saved my life, but saved everything important to me. For that, I shall be eternally in your debt."

Griffin recovered from his shock and thanked Mr. Dent. After the happy couple left the apartment, he and his uncle compared their incredible new timepieces. They both felt like true gentlemen!

Snodgrass opened his watch and set the time. But in doing so, his smile faded. He turned to Griffin and said, "My goodness, it's nearly three o'clock. We must get you to the train station."

Griffin's heart sank. He couldn't believe that it was time to go back home to America. He thought of the school year that was about to start, returning to the same horrible bullying he faced every year. Although the adventures over the summer had made him feel much more capable of defending himself, he dreaded the end of his trip.

Griffin and his uncle didn't say anything as Griffin went to get his suitcase, but they each knew how the other was feeling. It was going to be hard to say good-bye.

Suddenly there was another knock at the door. Outside was a boy in a bright red uniform. Griffin saw that he carried a telegram in his hand.

"Telegram for Mr. Griffin Sharpe," the boy said.

Griffin signed the acceptance form with a puzzled frown. Who could possibly be sending him a telegram?

His uncle gave the delivery boy a tip and closed the door. Griffin opened the letter and read:

Mr. Griffin Sharpe
221A Baker Street
London, England

Dear Mr. Sharpe,

It is with great regret that I inform you that your parents have been reported missing. On July 30th, investigators were alerted to an incident at your Boston residence. Upon arriving, there was evidence of a struggle, and Mr. and Mrs. Sharpe were nowhere to be found.

The police are baffled and have assigned every available investigator to the case. I encourage you to use caution when returning to America, for there was a threatening note left on the premises that mentioned you by name and was signed with the initials N.M.

Please seek me out upon your return.

Yours sincerely,

John H. Andover, Attorney

Griffin stared at the letter with a dawning sense of horror. There was no mistake about who had kidnapped his parents.

Nigel Moriarty had exacted his revenge!

Rupert Snodgrass read the note with a grim expression. Then he turned to Griffin and said, "We won't let this crime go unpunished, Griffin. I'll make immediate arrangements to travel with you to America. We'll find your parents and bring Nigel Moriarty to justice!"

And as Griffin rose from where he was sitting, with Nigel Moriarty's ebony swordstick clutched firmly in his hand, he knew with absolute certainty that his battle with the terrible villain was far from over.

A few hours later Griffin Sharpe and Rupert Snodgrass, the greatest detectives in London, boarded a ship for Boston. The rumpled detective with his brown bowler led a beautiful hound on a leash and was accompanied by his nephew, a young man of unique abilities who carried an unusual walking stick and walked with a limp.

And as they walked up the gangplank, the city was left unprotected.

There were eyes watching them as they left the dock, the glittering, intelligent eyes of an old spider that was forever spinning its web.

Professor James Moriarty chuckled quietly. Then, as his

steam-powered wheelchair rolled slowly away from the docks, he hummed a quiet tune. He felt happy, happier than he had in ages now that Sherlock Holmes had retired, and Snodgrass and Sharpe were out of the way.

His plan was working perfectly.

HOW SHARPE ARE YOU?

See if you can answer the following questions without checking the book. If you can get them all right, you're on your way to becoming the next Griffin Sharpe!

1. When we first meet Griffin, we find out that he notices everything. What are some of the things he does when he feels nervous?

2. Many people think that Big Ben is the name of the Westminster Clock Tower. What does Big Ben actually refer to?

3. Griffin takes a cab ride to a place called the Limehouse Docks. When he enters a store filled with fireworks, the Chinese woman who runs it greets him using the Chinese word for hello. Can you remember what she said?

4. Rupert Snodgrass has made many inventions that are similar to devices that we have today. His Snodgrass Falsehood Detector and his Snodgrass Super Finder are things that exist in our modern age. What do we call them today?

5. In the Sherlock Holmes stories, Professor Moriarity is

often referred to as the "Napoleon of Crime." Why do you think he was called that? Bonus question: Nigel Moriarty referred to himself as La Salle. Do you know who he was?

6. In Victorian England, people hired horses and buggies to get from place to place. Today, we call cars that do the same thing *taxis*. What were they commonly called back then?

7. What was Griffin's father's job? How do you think it affected Griffin's beliefs?

8. Rupert Snodgrass is not a Christian. How do you think that affected Griffin? How do you think Christians should act around nonbelievers?

9. Griffin's faith in God is a big part of his life. How do you think it affected the way he looked at people who needed his help?

10. Some people believe that the Loch Ness Monster is real. In this story, it's actually a submarine. What was it about the submarine that made it look so much like a monster?

11. Sometimes we can be so concerned with ourselves and the way we look to others that we forget about other people's feelings. Do you think Sherlock Holmes should have told Rupert that he couldn't find his dog sooner? Why or why not?

12. Rupert Snodgrass named his robot Watts. Why do you think he chose that name?

13. For many years, Rupert Snodgrass hated living next door to Sherlock Holmes. Have you ever felt jealous of other people's talents or abilities?

14. God gives us different gifts. If you were to help Griffin and his uncle solve crimes, what do you think you'd have to

offer? What part of their adventures would you look forward to the most?

Extra Credit

You can be a detective in your own home! Ask a brother, sister, or friend to play. Take turns hiding something somewhere, and then provide clues on how to find it. It's a great way to test your observation skills and see how well you match up to Griffin Sharpe!

GRIFFIN SHARPE
MINI-MYSTERIES

THE COMPOSER'S WILL

A Griffin Sharpe Mini-Mystery

Griffin Sharpe limped into the elegant living room, his walking stick making a small clicking noise as it tapped against the hardwood floor.

"Master Sharpe, so good of you to come!" said a young woman. Griffin smiled and shook her gloved hand.

Beatrice Thompson was pretty and about five years older than he was. Her eyes were large and brown, and she had an interesting brooch at her neck. Griffin saw that it was carved with the likeness of a honeybee.

"I like your brooch," he said. *"Apis mellifera,* correct?"

The girl appeared confused. Griffin smiled and said, "It's the scientific name for *honeybee.*"

She brightened. "Oh yes," she said, her hand going to the brooch. "My father gave it to me when I was young. He always said I was his little Bea."

At the mention of her father, Griffin noticed her expression change. Her lip trembled, and her eyes filled with tears. Griffin felt sorry for her and offered her his clean handkerchief. Since the incident with Mrs. Dent, he'd found it useful to carry one when dealing with clients who were involved in a difficult or emotional case.

"Thank you," she said, taking the handkerchief and dabbing at her eyes. "It's been hard not having my father around anymore."

Griffin gave her a compassionate look. Then he said gently, "I understand that there was some trouble with his estate?"

The girl nodded. "Yes, you see, my father was a great composer and had saved quite a fortune over the years. After he died, there were a lot of arguments about who was entitled to his money because he didn't leave a will. My uncle feels he's entitled to all of it and, if he has his wishes, he would see me thrown out into the streets."

"And where is your uncle now?"

"He's at a law office in London. If he can make his case to a barrister, he feels that he could have this house and my father's fortune handed to him within twenty-four hours!"

Griffin considered the situation. Then he asked, "Did your father express his dying wishes in any way? Did you have any conversations with him about what he wanted done with his money?"

"No, but he did give me this before he died," she said, handing Griffin a piece of paper. "It was the last piece of music he ever composed. He wrote it on his deathbed, and it's a terrible shame that he never had the chance to finish it."

Griffin saw that it was a piece of music titled "To Whom My Treasure Goes." It was a very short piece of music. Griffin saw only three notes positioned on the musical staff.

A single chord.

"Rest assured, Miss Beatrice," Griffin said smiling. "The fortune is yours."

How did Griffin know?

Turn to page 195 at the back of the book for the answer.

THE CASE OF THE TEXAS SHARPSHOOTER

A Griffin Sharpe Mini-Mystery

Griffin Sharpe and his uncle, the famous crime-fighting inventor Rupert Snodgrass, were attending a special event by invitation of the Queen. Ace McQuarrie, a gunslinger from Texas, was putting on a shooting exhibition, proving himself the greatest sharpshooter in the world.

Griffin had barely slept for a week because he was so excited to see the event. And when the day finally arrived, he was relieved to see that it had dawned crisp and clear without the slightest chance of rain.

After arriving at the palace, Griffin made his way to a row of reserved seats on the immense lawn. He and his uncle were dressed in their best clothes, and although his stiff new collar felt itchy, Griffin tried his best to ignore it. He glanced eagerly around the platform erected in front of him, hoping to get a glimpse of Mr. McQuarrie.

"They say he served with General Custer," Griffin whispered to his uncle.

"Custard? He served custard?" came his uncle's confused reply.

Griffin snickered. Sometimes he forgot that his uncle was British and didn't know American celebrities.

"Ladies and gentlemen," said a man in a fancy top hat. He waved his hands dramatically for silence as he walked onto the platform.

Griffin craned his neck to get a better view. He noticed that the stage was covered with stationary targets of various shapes and sizes. Some were large, and some were so small he wondered how anyone could be skillful enough to see them, let alone hit them with a bullet.

"It is my honor to introduce the fastest gun in the West. My friend Ace McQuarrie has bested the best, slapping leather with the quickest guns in Texas. What you're about to see is his most ambitious display of skill to date. Within the space of three seconds, he will destroy all of these targets on this stage, culminating with a perfect shot through the center of this card."

The man held up an ace of spades and tucked it into the brim of his hat. "I assure you that I am not concerned for my personal safety, for my friend Ace has never missed." Then he gulped theatrically and added for comedic effect, "Yet."

Ripples of laughter scattered through the crowd. Griffin noticed that even the Queen was smiling.

"So it is without further ado I introduce . . . Ace McQuarrie!"

A man clad in flashy buckskin and a tall, white cowboy hat climbed up onto the stage. Griffin clapped with the others. The man waved his big hat in appreciation, his white teeth sparkling from underneath his flowing blond moustache.

After a gracious nod to the Queen, he took his position. Griffin saw his hand poised over the side of his six-shooter, ready to fire.

The man in the top hat took out his timer. Then, in a loud voice, he boomed, "Ready, Ace?"

The cowboy nodded.

"One . . . two . . . three . . . GO!"

There was a burst of gunfire. One by one the targets exploded or ricocheted as the bullets hit them. Griffin watched as a pan clanged, a bell rang, three plates exploded, and a thimble, almost too small to see, flew off of a fence railing.

And last, just as the stopwatch hit three seconds, the card from the man's top hat flew from his head and fluttered to the ground. The crowd shouted in amazement as the man held up the card, a perfect hole drilled through the center of the ace.

Ace McQuarrie doffed his hat to the thunderous applause. But Rupert Snodgrass noticed that his nephew was the only one who wasn't clapping.

"What's the matter, Griffin?" Snodgrass asked. "You weren't impressed?"

"I would have been," said Griffin, "if he hadn't cheated."

What did Griffin know?

Turn to page 195 at the back of the book for the answer.

ANSWERS TO GRIFFIN SHARPE
MINI-MYSTERIES

ANSWER TO "THE COMPOSER'S WILL"

When Griffin saw the notes on the musical staff, he recognized exactly what they were: B E A. The letters formed the nickname Bea, short for Beatrice. When this was presented in court, the judge ruled in favor of Miss Thompson, and she was awarded the entirety of her father's estate.

ANSWER TO
"THE CASE OF THE TEXAS SHARPSHOOTER"

Griffin counted the shots. One at the pan, one at the bell, three at the plates, one at the target, and one at the card. Seven shots. Considering that the man held only a six-shooter, such a feat was impossible. Shortly after the contest, Griffin followed the clues and found evidence of a second shooter hidden behind a tree, the source of the extra shot.

MRS. TOTTINGHAM'S
DELICIOUS SCONE RECIPE

(Griffin Sharpe's favorite)

(The following is a recipe passed down from the original Mrs. Tottingham. Her great-granddaughter Eloise assures me that it is exactly the same one Griffin Sharpe loved so much.)

- 2 cups of flour
- 1 tablespoon of baking powder
- 1/2 teaspoon of salt
- 3 tablespoons of sugar
- 5 tablespoons cold, unsalted butter cut into cubes
- 1 cup of milk

Sift together flour, baking powder, salt, and sugar. Cut in the butter until the dough looks crumbly. Add in milk and stir gently.

Press dough onto lightly floured surface. Cut into squares and then half them into triangle shapes.

Bake on an ungreased cookie sheet at 400 degrees Fahrenheit for 15 to 20 minutes.

Lemon Icing

Juice of 1/2 of a squeezed lemon
2 cups of powdered sugar
Zest of one lemon
Teaspoon of vanilla
Milk to thin as needed

Mix together and drizzle over cooled scones. Serve with a pot of hot tea and your favorite Griffin Sharpe mystery book. Best eaten next to a roaring fire!

THE **FUTURE DOOR**

Don't miss out on more of
Griffin's exciting adventures
in book 2 of the
No Place Like Holmes series.

PROLOGUE

London
1903

M rs. Hudson wiped her hands on her apron as she hurried to the front door of 221 Baker Street. The delicious scent of roasting chicken and rosemary wafted from behind her as she rushed out of the kitchen to answer the persistent knocking.

"Half a moment," she called irritably. If there were one thing she didn't like, it was being interrupted when in the middle of preparing a meal for her tenants. After pausing to tuck a few stray hairs back beneath her cap, she opened the door. To her surprise, a pretty young woman dressed in boy's clothing was standing on the doorstep.

"May I help you?" Mrs. Hudson asked suspiciously. She scanned the woman's attire, taking in her dyed wool jacket, trousers, and newsboy's cap. Somehow, in spite of the unflattering clothing, the girl still managed to look feminine.

"You must be Mrs. Hudson! My name is Charlotte Pepper. It's so very nice to meet you," she said, extending her hand. Mrs. Hudson was taken aback for a moment, but then, seeing no other polite way around it, shook her offered hand. Women didn't usually shake hands. It was considered a manly gesture and indelicate.

"And what can I do for you, Miss Pepper?" Mrs. Hudson asked.

"I heard that you were looking for a new tenant and have come to inquire about the apartment. I don't need to see it. All that we need to discuss is the price. How much rent do you require?"

Mrs. Hudson noticed that when she spoke, Charlotte Pepper didn't make eye contact, but instead glanced everywhere else, including the hallway behind her. A smile played around the woman's full lips and her huge, brown eyes danced with excitement. Turning back to the landlady she said, "Is it indeed the apartment of the famous Sherlock Holmes?"

"Until recently, yes," Mrs. Hudson replied with a hint of annoyance. Ever since her favorite tenant had departed, she'd had no end of "lookie loos" that had showed up, wanting to catch a glimpse of the great detective's apartment.

"Miss, ah . . . Pepper," Mrs. Hudson said with a hint of annoyance, "I don't wish to be rude, but the apartment in question is quite expensive." She glanced at the young woman's shabby, unflattering clothing. "Mr. Holmes was an accomplished detective with a reliable income, and I mean for my new tenant to meet the same qualifications."

If Charlotte Pepper was offended by the remark, she didn't show it.

"Well, I assure you that money is no object," she stated. "Simply name your price, and I shall pay it . . ." Mrs. Hudson started to reply, but Charlotte interrupted her, holding up a finger.

". . . And as your newest tenant, you should know two things about me. First of all, I am exceedingly punctual. You could say that time itself is one of the most important things to me."

She paused to smile even more widely.

"And second, I am absolutely without question, the biggest fan of Sherlock Holmes who ever lived. I am a bit of an amateur detective myself and will treat the premises with the utmost care and respect. I am clean, decent, and well-mannered. In other words, the perfect tenant."

She reached into her jacket pocket and removed the largest wad of British currency that Mrs. Hudson had ever seen. After pressing it into the landlady's startled hand, she stepped past her into the hallway.

"I believe it's just down here to the left, correct?"

Mrs. Hudson, feeling completely flummoxed, followed in her new tenant's wake. *Another detective at Baker Street?* she thought. First, Mr. Holmes, then Mr. Snodgrass, and now, this precocious female? And just who did Charlotte Pepper think she was, bossing her around; not asking, but telling her that she was to accept her as her tenant automatically.

But Mrs. Hudson didn't express her feeling aloud. For one of the first times in her life, the landlady was left feeling absolutely speechless. And she couldn't help thinking that her old tenant, Mr. Sherlock Holmes, would have enjoyed seeing it happen for once.

As she closed the front door behind her, Mrs. Hudson failed to notice the disreputable character who was standing beneath the gaslight on the opposite side of the street. The lumpy man stared after the departing women with a twisted grin.

"Right on schedule," he whispered. Then, with hardly a backward glance, the man hurried into the shadows to report what he'd seen to his waiting master.